It's Not Love, It's Just Paris

Also by Patricia Engel

Vida

IT'S NOT LOVE,
IT'S JUST PARIS

PATRICIA ENGEL

Grove Press
New York

Published simultaneously in Canada
Printed in the United States of America

FIRST EDITION

ISBN-13: 978-0-8021-2151-6

Grove Press
an imprint of Grove/Atlantic, Inc.
154 West 14th Street
New York, NY 10011

Distributed by Publishers Group West

www.groveatlantic.com

13 14 15 16   10 9 8 7 6 5 4 3 2 1

Always for my parents

"In love, hold on to what is."

—Albert Camus

It's Not Love, It's Just Paris

1

The first person to call it the House of Stars was Séraphine's husband, Théophile, a drunk who often passed out in the entrance court before making it to the front door. He'd say that, from his cheek-to-the-cobblestone view, all he saw were faint lights, like stars, in the bedroom windows, and no matter the hour there were always stars out on our stretch of rue du Bac, which is also how Séraphine's place got a reputation among others for being a house that never sleeps.

I'd just met her when she told me Théo carried on an affair with her sister, Charlotte, the whole time they were married, but he'd chosen Séraphine for his wife because she was the one who inherited the de la Roque fortune. Everyone knew about Théo and Charlotte's romance, but back then people were more strategic in their marrying.

"It was the fashion," Séraphine said, and believe me, a lot of things you'd never expect were *the fashion*. Soon after my arrival, I asked what happened to Théophile because I hadn't yet met him but always saw his hat resting on the chest in the front foyer as if he were lost somewhere in the house. Séraphine rearranged herself among her bed pillows and lit a cigarette before sighing, "My Théo suicided himself seventeen years ago. The writer who lived across the way had done the same a month before. It was the fashion."

Séraphine was a countess. Around the house, and even around Paris, people still kept track of that stuff even though titles went out with the Revolution. I was told by the guy who recommended me as a tenant that I should address her as Madame la Comtesse or just plain Countess if I planned on sticking to English, but I couldn't utter either without feeling I was part of a performance. So, within hours of my arrival I asked if I could call her by her first name instead. Her kohl-lined eyes expanded to reveal their inner pink membranes and she took a while to respond. I was thinking this sort of friendliness might have been a grave mistake and wondered if there was a way to reverse it when Séraphine finally cleared her throat and smiled with what, using her frown lines as evidence, I took to be her first in years.

"Very well, Leticia. You may call me Séraphine. If you *insist*."

Soon all the girls started calling her Séraphine, too, even those who'd been residents for years already and had always addressed her formally. Her grandson Loic tried to rectify my disgrace, saying it was rude of us to be so familiar and we should at least address her as Madame since we were all guests in Séraphine's house, which wasn't really true given that we paid good money to live there, in American dollars no less—a year's rent in full, up front. But it was too late; the order of the house had already shifted.

Princess Diana had died while I was on the night flight from Newark to Paris. The taxi driver tossed *Le Figaro* with the headline and picture of the tunnel crash across my lap and drove me from Charles de Gaulle over to the Seventh. I remembered watching her wedding on television with my mother when I was a kid and it didn't feel like so long ago, but now that was just a story people would tell, and instead of happily ever after, it would be *And the princess and her lover died together in Paris. The End.* The news of her death made me feel old and brought on a sharp longing for my mother, who'd turned her back from me at the airport so I wouldn't see the shine of her tears. The taxi driver let me keep the newspaper. He'd bought multiple copies, he said, figuring they'd be worth something because it's not every day a princess dies. I tucked it into the back of my jeans and dragged my two suitcases off the sidewalk, across the courtyard to the countess's house, and into the foyer. Nobody turned up when I rang the bell.

Like Séraphine, the House of Stars must have been very beautiful once. You could see the allure and majesty under the costume of Persian rugs, marble floors, molded ceilings, enormous chandeliers, and gilded mirrors. But if you looked closer you'd see the rugs were darkened with age, spotted with cigarette stains, worn with high-heel holes. The marble floor, chipped and decades overdue for a polishing. The moldings, cracked with cherubs missing heads or wings, the mirrors fogged over, their frames tarnished, the chandeliers missing crystals and bulbs. Then there were the decorative details: wooden furniture with mother-of-pearl and enamel inlays that were Louis something or other, chests and tiny tables holding figurines, and miniature silver boxes—the sort of stuff you'd see at any garage sale back home. And that bouquet of old tobacco, lingering despite all those little glass bowls of lavender potpourri.

A voice called and I followed it down the short hall off the foyer.

And then I saw her: Séraphine, propped up by a mound of white cushions in a large mahogany sleigh bed floating at the center of the room over a floor layered with carpets. Lace curtains shrouded glass doors that opened onto the back garden. She was dressed in a white bed gown, her legs covered by an airy duvet, looking porcelain with what was left of her long, colorless hair swiped into a tight bun. Pearls drooped off her ears, her thin lips were covered in a runny red pigment, and her light eyes were lined with a dark gunk that was her trademark and probably the reason for her cataracts. Even in bed, fat like a panda, she was an elegant sort of lady, just like the younger Séraphine staring back at her from the framed photographs lining the yellowed walls, and I often wondered what her husband didn't see in her.

By then, Séraphine was almost ninety and hadn't left her room in three years; a vestige that came with the house. The maids called her the maharani because doctors, friends, and the bits of the world that mattered to Séraphine came to her when summoned. They said she would have to be bulldozed out if any of her descendants were to have their way and try to sell the house, as I soon learned her own daughter was hoping to do.

When I asked Séraphine why she decided to rent out rooms in her house, she explained that before it was the House of Stars it was the House of Felines. Théo, who was the obsessive type, had collected his way up to fifty or so of some rare breed of Siamese, and each room, which now boarded a girl, once housed five or six cats, plus a few favorites who had free reign of the estate. Théo treated the cats like curios and spent his days visiting each of them, brushing them and clipping their nails, whispering in Russian because Théo was Russian in his former life, rumored to be Jewish, though it was never mentioned, because the de la Roque family wanted people to think they were thoroughly French and Catholic, throwing around that old proverb that a good name is worth more than a golden belt. The maids said that was also the reason Séraphine never took Théo's giveaway of a last name and why he was so taken with the writer across the street who was also Russian and Jewish in some capacity.

One day Séraphine got fed up with the cats. She said she couldn't do anything about Théophile sleeping with her sister like it was his God-given right, but she could evict the cats because it was her house, inherited from her father who favored her as his firstborn. She'd wanted to pack up the cats and send them to live with the prostitutes and bums in the Bois de Boulogne, but those cats were each worth a small bundle, so she found herself a cat broker and sold him the lot for a lump sum. He came to collect them with a van full of cages one evening while Théo was out drinking. When he sobered up the next day and saw the cats were gone, Théo had a breakdown and Séraphine was certain he never really forgave her. It was Théophile's idea to fill the rooms with girls now that the cats were gone. They started out with two, then three, and worked their way up to eight. She said Théo found keeping young girls just as amusing as keeping cats. The maids murmured that for all their blue blood and this property, one of the few remaining hôtels particuliers on the Left Bank, the de la Roque family was broke. The countess discovered an easy income in housing allegedly well-bred debutante borders and plenty of parents eager to pay a onetime noblewoman to supervise their daughters en séjour.

I was the only new girl that season. There was a long waiting list to live in the house, and a girl was considered only if personally recommended as I was by a former Nouveau Roman professor who was tenuously related to Théophile. Each girl was given her own private room on the second and third floors while Séraphine lived downstairs. Her grandsons, Loic and Gaspard, the sons of her only daughter, Nicole, had an apartment in the smaller west wing of the house, accessed through a separate entrance or through a narrow hideaway passage under the stairs leftover from the war. Séraphine assigned me to the bedroom above hers at the top of the staircase on the second level, a tunnel-like space with a set of double doors opening onto the corridor and a pair of glass panels on the opposite wall leading to a small balcony overlooking the terrace and back garden. Within it, a single bed with a limp mattress pushed into a corner, a small desk, a folding chair, a black lacquer dresser missing a few glass knobs, and a red velvet love seat with sunken cushions and splitting wooden legs.

Even though there were three maids, Violeta, Flora, and Mara, Portuguese sisters whose mother was the rarely seen concierge living in a little apartment just inside the entrance court, and Loic and Gaspard were supposed to be the house managers, I'd arrived when everybody was taking their lunch. Thus no one came along to help drag my bags upstairs or to show me where things were, like the kitchen or the common phone, which only received incoming calls, or to tell me the toilet was on one end of the hall while the tiled washroom with a curtainless bath, handheld shower, and sink were down the other end.

I'd opened the balcony doors to clear out the stale air and was kneeling on my bedroom floor, pulling clothes from a suitcase, when I noticed twin pairs of sandals in the doorway belonging to two girls staring down at me as if I were a raccoon rummaging through a trash pile. I don't have sisters, just two brothers—one older and one younger—I hadn't had many girlfriends at school and felt like I knew my way around books better than people. I was twenty years old, graduated from a top university with honors, two years ahead of schedule in life, but still a social novice. And these girls, Tarentina and Giada, as they introduced themselves, came off as a fearsome twosome, their dirty blonde hair in tangled bobs, black bras peeking from the tops of their nearly identical knee-grazing floral dresses and similar firm round breasts that Loic later told me they'd purchased together during last year's Easter holiday in Tarentina's hometown of Rio—it was *the fashion.*

Giada, slightly shorter, leaned on the door frame, her lips in a permanent pout, while her friend asked who I was and where I came from with a quasi-British twang I'd learn was standard among the Swiss boarding-school set. I told them my name was Leticia but I went by Lita and I was American. By their faces I could tell they did not believe me.

"What are your last names?" Tarentina asked.

"Del Cielo. It's the only one I've got."

She smiled, though not warmly.

"That sounds like a stage name. What's your blood?"

"My blood?"

"Your lineage," she sighed, already bored with me. "Your country. You know, what are you *made of?*"

"Colombian."

"Indian, I presume." She turned to Giada. "That explains the jungle face."

In fact I was named for a jungle city in the Amazon on the shared frontiers of Colombia, Brazil, and Peru. I didn't come out of the jungle, but my mother did, found abandoned on a road and turned over to some nuns who took her back to the capital. Back then, indigenous babies were nearly unadoptable, and instead of turning her over to an orphanage, the nuns raised my mother in the convent. I didn't feel like explaining any of that, so all I said was, "I guess it does."

"Well, Loic asked me to tell you he's on his way. He usually does the welcoming. We'll chat more once you settle in."

They departed with a "Ciao Ciao," their sandals flapping down the stairs over their soft laughter, until they were out the front door. Dread spread over me. I'd hoped to live on my own in Paris, scouring classifieds in a secondhand *FUSAC*, circling affordable studio apartment listings, but my father had insisted he'd only let me live abroad if I had company, a respectable witness to my existence. The House of Stars was the compromise I now began to regret.

A short while later, Loic, gangly in his gingham shirt, pressed trousers, and prematurely wrinkled face, tapped on my door and introduced himself.

"So sorry not to have been here when you arrived. I had an emergency of sorts. Well, a friend had an emergency."

I stood up to greet him, shaking his bony hand.

"Have you had a look around the house yet?"

"Yes. It's . . . nice. I met your grandmother and some of the other girls. Giada and—"

"Tarentina."

He stared at me, his eyes a watery blue.

"The first day is always the hardest."

I forced a smile.

"I'm just tired. From the travel. The time change."

"Why don't you take a break from your unpacking and join me outside for some fresh air." He held out his hand as if luring me off a ledge.

Loic's idea of fresh air was a cigarette. We sat on the front steps of the house, his knobby knee gliding against the blue jeans I'd pulled on the day before back in New Jersey as my father shouted from downstairs that if I didn't hurry, I'd miss my flight. Loic offered me a Lucky Strike from his pack. I wasn't a smoker but I'd smoked plenty with Ajax, my childhood best friend, who was a real fiend, especially when he was coming off drugs. I might never have come to Paris if not for Ajax, whose real name was Andrew Jackson, just like the president. We were early nerds together, thrown together in the exile of the "gifted" classes and Saturday enrichment programs at the local college. He was traumatized into being an achiever since he found out that his father, whom he'd thought was dead, was actually a dentist with another family across town and Ajax's mother had been his receptionist. We went to the same school as his half siblings, and Ajax decided to excel in class to make them look like the losers.

Ajax and his mother lived in a tiny apartment above the liquor store, and my family lived in a professionally decorated mansion, but he still thought we were minority trash because his mother raised him on the myth that they were the long-lost cousins of the Kennedys. His mother left him alone a lot, and afternoons, when we were meant to be studying at the library, we'd hide out in his room watching Bones Brigade videos and planning our destiny as supercool adults. Neither of us really fit into our whitewashed town of monograms and country club memberships, but I didn't mind much because Ajax always said community is just conformity with a rose behind its ear.

Ajax got me into skateboarding and one day took my dare to try a hand plant in our drained swimming pool and broke his back, which took him out of ninth grade for four months. When they weaned him off the painkillers, Ajax, who now walked like an old man, made friends with the liquor store gang outside his door and landed on heroin. He was currently in jail for trying to kill his mother. I'd never visited him but I once sent him a box of books he'd lent me over the years. Most of them were stolen from the library or local bookstore anyway. They were sexy books. Books about Europe and elsewhere, people living uncharted lives—the kind of people we both wanted to be after high school. Then, Ajax said, we'd really start living. But the box of books was returned to me, so I took it to his apartment hoping to leave it with his mother, but she had moved, and when I asked down at the liquor store, nobody knew where she'd gone.

Maybe it was the rotated yellowing teeth, the hollow cheeks, stork-thin arms, or the way Loic held his cigarette between his middle and ring finger, but my memories of Ajax built an instant bridge of familiarity between us. Maybe it was his eyes, pale and beckoning. Maybe it's just that lonely attracts lonely.

Loic was the kind of guy who'd drive down Avenue Foch in his Mini and pick up a young hooker only to give her free money and offer to help her find a decent job somewhere. He really did that, about once a week, but I was the only one who knew, because I've always been the sort of person people find it easy to tell their secrets to. The truth is I'm very quiet out loud, shy like an escargot, saving my chatter for the privacy of my own mind, and I'm only talky like this when I'm still trying to understand what things mean to me.

I took the cigarette Loic offered me that afternoon thinking it was a good way to christen this new life. Loic didn't say much, not even when I broke into a coughing fit after my first drag. He looked over his sharp shoulder and, through his smoky smile, as if he could read my weariness and fears, said, "Don't worry, Lita. You're going to be very happy here. I promise."

*   *   *

My father says you can't go anywhere without leaving something behind. It sounds better in Spanish—less simple, although my father is a simple man. He's a tycoon now but he was illiterate until he was nineteen and says poverty can't be covered by a new suit, which also sounds much better in Spanish, but you get the picture.

My mother, as I said, was found in the jungle. She could be Brazilian or Peruvian just as easily as Colombian since most national lines drawn through the rainforest are only observed by maps. She might be mestiza or pure Indian, though we don't know her tribe—Bora, Yagua, or Ticuna—it's hard to say, since being dropped in the city was her first displacement. She's got thick black hair strong enough to strangle someone, which I inherited along with her straight brows and long eyes that stretch to my ears. Alligator eyes are what my brothers call them, because they got our father's eyes, small and round like coffee beans, and his condor nose. My older brother, Santi, would say that unless you hang with Lévi-Strauss, chances are we don't look like anyone you know. We're sand colored, tall and lean with angular butts. My father says it's from generations of hunger and malnutrition that came before us, but that can't be verified, because, like my mother, Papi was also abandoned. When he was six or seven his father packed him with a bundle of arepas and left him alone in a Bogotá park. It was sunset before he realized his father wasn't coming back for him. He went to the safest place he could think of to wait out the night, a church, and spent the next five years sleeping on its steps among the derelicts and street kids until he observed a man who came for daily Mass and, figuring the guy must be halfway decent, one day followed him home. Papi doesn't like to get into details, but sleeping on the church steps was pretty dangerous and he got all the propositions you'd imagine a twelve-year-old homeless boy would get.

The man my father followed turned out to be an ironworker, and he agreed to let Papi work for him in exchange for food and a place to sleep. Eight years later, the man, Santiago, sent Papi to repair the fence around a convent on the city periphery. That's where he met my mother—an eighteen-year-old nun in training. It sounds kind of telenovela escandaloso, but they fell in love and my mother became pregnant. She didn't have the nerve to tell the nuns, so she just ran away with my father, whose name is Beto, leaving a note for the nuns confessing everything. He had a dream to get them both to the United States, where he heard poor people had more of a chance. It took them a while to find a way out of the country, but a rich guy whose window bars he installed had prize Doberman puppies that needed escorts for their emigration to New York. My father begged for the job. The rich guy had friends in high places who could take care of the passports, but neither of my parents had last names, so my father went back to the church where he'd spent his urchin years and a young priest agreed to marry him and my mother and sign a document vouching for their existence. That's when my parents picked out their own last name: del Cielo, because they figured the only father they had now was God.

The only sad part is that their baby was born dead. They called her Eden. Years later, my parents took us back to Colombia to visit the nuns and show them their young family. Mami had been writing them for years, first about her new life in Los Estados and the three children that were born there. We went out to the convent garden where my parents met and had an improvised funeral for Eden. I was only five and didn't realize what was going on until the Mother

Superior put a thin gold chain around my neck that she said had been meant for Eden, who was now my spirit sister. I wore it until it broke off a few years ago and my mother placed it in a special rosewood box beside her bed, next to her altar of favorite saints.

I can tell you all about the Great American Crossover because my parents never shut up about the early days. How they made it to JFK Airport, delivered the puppies, and Papi called a Jackson Heights connection provided by Santiago who found him a job sweeping in a warehouse, and one for Mami cleaning bathrooms at an elementary school. She'd been teaching my father to read Spanish, but now they had to start from nothing and learn English together. You'd never know it, because my father hardly has an accent now. Of course it wasn't always this way. As Papi says, all of us are living many lives at once.

My father also says that every person gets a vision once in their life that holds the key to their future. I know it sounds like Disney talk but he swears by it and says that after a year as a Queens janitor he dreamed about the day his father left him at the park, saw his weathered crying face, and heard him sob, "Perdoname, hijo, perdoname," because his father had six other kids and was ashamed he couldn't afford to feed them all. He handed Papi the pack of arepas saying, "This will help you fight the hunger for a while."

Papi shook my mother awake.

"Caridad, we're going to start an arepa factory!"

It sounds funny now. And when business magazines do articles on my father because he's now known as the King of Latin Foods, they always get a kick out of that anecdote. But it's true. Papi says arepas, just white corn flour, peasant food, are the heart of any Colombian diet. So my mother started making them and my father started selling them on the streets of Queens during the daylight hours, working the nightshift sweeping. A year later he had enough cash to open a kiosk, and a few years after that, when Papi's English was good enough, he managed to convince a young banker to give him a loan. With it, they opened their first bakery and then the first factory, which eventually grew to national and now global distribution of all the cornerstones of Latin American household cuisine.

And my mother? They don't call her Our Lady of New Jersey for nothing. Since she and my father had it so rough when they landed in the United States, my mother was determined to help out as many new arrivals as she could and word got around. When someone arrived, they called her or just showed up at our door and my mother would bring them in, give them clothes, groceries, listen to their stories, and set them up with a job. Mami had built an intricate network of those she'd helped over the years who now had their own businesses. She was a one-woman embassy, getting the new arrivals to doctors who treated at a discount, lawyers willing to help with their papers, tutoring their children so they wouldn't get railroaded into the slow classes in school. She was godmother to about thirty kids already and the namesake of a dozen others. She drove an old baby blue Mercedes and still wore her fat whip of a braid down to her waist, never a drop of makeup, and the same mochila she carried with her on that flight with the dogs out of Colombia.

My father says he only moved us out to a fancy New Jersey suburb because he had a dream of owning acres, a house with many rooms so nobody he knew would ever be left without a place to sleep, and this was the closest thing my parents had known to paradise. There were always extra plates at the dinner table—water added to the soup, is what Mami would say—always a bed freshly made, waiting for the next guest, be it for a night, a week, or a month. On Sundays after church, our house was Grand Central

Station for Tristate Colombians, people passing through to say hello, celebrating successes or quietly relaying bad news, dropping off pasteles, buñuelitos, chicharrónes, and albóndingas, any little gesture of gratitude for my parents.

I thought this was how all families operated until Ajax started coming over and mocked our clan, saying, "When immigrants get money they turn their mansions into refugee camps."

But my older brother, Santi, explained to me that Ajax probably acquired that line at home and the only thing people resent more than poor immigrants are wealthy ones:

"Remember, hermanita, the Brown American Dream is the White American Nightmare."

I never thought much of any of this until I moved into Séraphine's house. There, it was as if everyone carried their family history in their pocket, bragging about bloodlines, waving the family crest rings on their fingers. The paperwork to live in the House of Stars was more detailed than a college application, asking for the names and nationalities of grandparents and great-grandparents. I didn't have anything to put in those spaces. Séraphine had been forced to grow lenient over the years, though. She said there were hardly any real blue bloods anymore; immigration, Communism, dictatorships, and little countries gaining independence did away with nobility and name privilege. Now, in the era of "le Self-Made," a sort of charlatanism in her view, she lamented that any nobody off the street could come into the opportunities, money, and property that used to be afforded to the few of a certain birthright. According to Séraphine, all of us girls residing in the House of Stars were part of the fresh and hungry newly moneyed international breed that was turning France into a resigned colony of our pleasures. We were the *greenbloods*, full of equity, pedigree unknown.

2

Loic was an actor, though he'd never taken an acting class or performed anywhere. He said just because an artist isn't actively creating doesn't mean their time is without artistic value; if you want to create art you've got to *live* art, and he was in a period of creative fermentation, which sounded to me like a whole lot of nothing, but Loic was almost thirty, so I figured he knew something about life that I didn't.

The day after my arrival, he took me on a tour of the neighborhood, pointing out the locales that made up my new vie quotidienne. The pharmacies, the boulanger with the best baguette, the post office around the corner, the tabac with the cheapest cigarettes, the wine shop, the cleaners, the public pool, the Italian restaurant up the street where the girls of the house ate a few times a week because they were friends with the waiters. He showed me the nearby métros and bus stops, bought me my first carte orange, showed me the cheap French grocer and the expensive one where they sold American brands. He brought me to the best local pub—Claude's, nested behind the Odéon, and pointed out La Verité, the bar for men where Gaspard worked that one could only enter with a secret password.

He led me across Saint Germain to the language school where I'd start classes the following week. That's how I got myself to Paris. I'd majored in Romance languages and deferred my acceptance to a graduate program in international relations in exchange for a year in Paris I claimed would give me a linguistic edge in my intended career in diplomacy. It was a decoy, though. I wanted more than what I let on. Sometimes it was to be a professor, a journalist, a novelist, a cultural anthropologist, or all these things at once. I was only certain that I wanted a fluid, creative life. And academics proved an easy scaffold. I was a practical girl, after all, raised among survivalists.

The House of Stars was full of self-identifying artists. I didn't know how many of them were inborn or if it was just that, in Paris, art was contagious. Séraphine declared herself an authentic artiste because she once performed with la Comédie-Française and painted very well before her fingers contorted from arthritis. She wrote poems for lovers and was an excellent equestrienne, which she maintained was an art form, as was throwing good parties and keeping an eclectic group of friends.

"Art is a matter of the spirit, chérie," she'd say. It wasn't that I was special—she called everyone chéri or chérie, and if you spent more than three minutes with her, you were bound to receive a fat dose of advice or philosophy.

I'd heard from Loic that Maribel, the rangy Spanish girl, was a painter, raised in conservatories and by parents who were famous artists who dressed like mimes in identical leotard ensembles and were the subject of coffee table books and museum retrospectives. At twenty-one, Maribel was primed for a promising career as the star of Beaux-Arts. I met her over breakfast. Every morning the maids set the dining room table with a spread of coffee, baguettes, and brioches, but I'd been shy those first days and remained in my room alone as I heard the laughter and chatter of the girls on the floor below. The first time I went down to join them, I found a seat at the end of the table between Naomi, the spider-thin Manhattanite, and petite and golden Dominique, the daughter of a French former model and the Lebanese founder of the Marpessa resorts lining the Mediterranean from Beirut to Saint-Tropez.

"Hi. I'm Lita," I tried a casual tone.

I dwarfed them in size, but the indifference on their faces made me feel quite small.

"She's the new girl," Tarentina told the table as if it weren't already clear. She sat at the head, wrapped in a silk robe and a boa of cigarette smoke.

There were a few small waves but no further introductions. I'd have to piece together their identities myself. Saira, the African girl, sat across from me and offered me one of the brioches in the basket between us. She lived on the third floor in the room directly above mine, and I'd already heard from Loic that she was the youngest child of an ousted dictator who was currently being treated for cancer in Casablanca.

"We were just talking about the news," Maribel said, turning to me. "Have you heard?"

I expected more details about the death of the princess, but that morning the girls were captivated by the story of an American who'd arrived from San Francisco the day before expressly for the occasion of his suicide, throwing himself on the Franklin D. Roosevelt métro tracks at the height of the evening rush, holding up the trains for hours.

"His mother said he'd never been to Paris before but he knew he wanted to die here. He wasn't sick. Not even remarkably depressed. He just wanted to live his dream of dying in Paris."

"What are they going to do with his body?" asked Camila, the other Colombian, an emerald-blood to whom Loic had already introduced me in the corridor assuming we'd be fast friends. She was also on the diplomacy track, having interned at The Hague, the U.N., and UNESCO, and was completing a law degree at Nanterre. Loic said all girls came to Paris under the guise of wanting to be fashion designers, models, chefs, or diplomats when all they were really after were husbands. That was before he knew diplomacy was my official career plan, too, but I wasn't offended, already accustomed to my brother Santi's position that diplomats are just professional dinner guests.

Loic pointed out that Camila and I were compatriots, but when I admitted I was born in the States, she wrinkled her nose and said, "So you can't really call yourself Colombian then, can you? Just a Colombogringa, at best." I could have argued that Queens, where I was born, is a Colombia satellite but was relieved she'd drawn a line between us so I wouldn't be burdened with having to get to know her. But Loic added that I was the heir to the Compa' Foods fortune and all of a sudden she was dying to be my friend.

"He's going to be buried back home," Maribel answered Camila. "He had enough sense to prepay his funeral and set money aside for the customs paperwork and shipping of his cadaver."

"That's so morbid," Naomi said, picking the layers off her croissant. Her room was also on the third floor, and I'd learn that she had a longtime boyfriend back home in addition to the Paris boyfriend I'd already seen floating around the house—an Egyptian boxer named Rachid who worked weekends at the Puces.

"It's not morbid. Everyone *dies,*" Maribel said. "I think it's romantic that he elected the scene of his death. When I die, I want it to be like that, a moment of my choosing."

"Don't be such an idiot." Tarentina tossed a brioche from her plate at Maribel. "It's your life, not a goddamn film."

Tarentina was the oldest and had been in the house the longest at five years, earning her way into the largest bedroom, down the hall from mine, with its own private bathroom. She'd changed schools nearly every semester of her residency, though she rarely went to class, devoting most of her time to two men and a few others she crammed in at intervals. Her preferred lovers, a famous English musician and an elderly almost-blind French art dealer living on rue Bonaparte who was always offering to adopt Tarentina so he'd have someone to leave his estate to. Her parents had died when she was a baby and her grandparents were dead now, too, so even though she was twenty-three, technically, since she was without family, she was still available.

I'd found out the orphan part the day before when she stopped by my room. I was at my desk writing a letter to my younger brother, Beto. We'd been writing each other for years, even while growing up in the same house. It had started at the suggestion of a therapist who thought it was a good way to draw Beto out of himself, but I told him it was because we didn't have ancestors, so it was on us to leave evidence of our existence in the written form.

I looked up as Tarentina announced, "I hear you're an orphan."

I shook my head. "I'm not."

"Why would the countess say you are then?"

"My parents are orphans. Maybe that's what she meant."

"You don't have to be embarrassed. I won't tell anyone if you are."

"That's my family." I pointed to a family photo I'd taped to the wall beside my bed taken at last year's Noche Buena party, the five of us standing before the Christmas tree.

Tarentina looked it over with a disaffected sigh.

"Too bad. All the best people in history are orphans. It's like magic, you know."

Later, when I told Loic about our encounter, he briefed me on Tarentina's not-so-secret history; her father killed her mother and then himself in what was deemed a "crime of passion," and even though she threw her fancy colonial last name around with pride, Loic said Tarentina's original last name was German because her father's father was not the full-blood sixth-generation Brazilian rancher she claimed, but a runaway Nazi.

I accepted the coffeepot from Saira, pouring into the cup placed on the chipped saucer before me. I sipped it. Bitter and diluted compared to the full-flavored coffee my father brewed in our house every morning. The girls went on about the virtues of suicide versus succumbing to illness or accidental death while I kept silent. I'd been raised around a crowded table and knew sometimes it's best not to compete for airtime and just wait your turn.

Giada eyed me from across the table.

"You look a bit like Tania. I mean, vaguely. You could be her cousin or something."

Since our first meeting, she'd softened toward me during our run-ins in the washroom where we took turns brushing our teeth over the sink. She told me her father held a minor political office in Rome, and after skidding out of an English boarding school, she was sent to Paris to be kept out of the Italian public eye and study pastry making, though she took pride in being a semiprofessional DJ groupie, rarely missing a night of Laurent Garnier at the superclubs on Les Champs and around la Bastille.

"Oh, I haven't met her yet." I said.

"That's because she's gone," Tarentina answered. "Tania lived in your room before you. She was here three years but she kept failing out of schools, so her parents finally made her go home to Istanbul."

"I heard she's getting engaged soon," Dominique informed them. She'd run into a friend of a friend in Porto Cervo who'd heard it from someone else, which led to resounding gasps.

"The bitch could have told us," Tarentina said. "Let's see if we're invited to the wedding."

"*If* there's a wedding," Camila added because Tania had apparently left a devoted boyfriend behind in Paris.

"I've never seen a guy love a girl the way he loved Tania except"—Giada turned to Saira—"except maybe the way your Stef loves you."

Saira had grown up in Geneva, and her family owned a staffed apartment on rue Royale, but Saira preferred to live in the house so she could continue seeing her boyfriend, her Stef, as Giada put it, a Belgian race-car driver who'd recently dropped out of the Formula One because of vision problems. Saira's family disapproved of him and only let her live in Séraphine's place because of the No Boys Allowed policy, though I quickly observed that the rule, like most of the others, was purely decorative, and Stef spent nearly every weekend in Saira's room.

"Stef's the only man in the world who is actually dying to get married," Dominique told me, but I was distracted by her heavy makeup and what looked like a pound of diamonds dripping from her ears, wrists, and in a heart-shaped pendant around her neck. "He proposes to her every other day."

"Only because he knows I'll never say yes," Saira laughed. "It would kill my father, and if not, my father would kill me."

"What about you, Lita? Did you leave a boyfriend back home?" asked Maribel, who'd moved from her breakfast to hand-rolling a cigarette on the tablecloth.

"No . . ."

"Are you sure?" Tarentina looked skeptical.

"No. I mean, no, there's nobody."

But there had been somebody. From long before. And he wasn't home but somewhere else, far away. Daniel. He was our Jordanian neighbor Abel's nephew and a surrogate son since Abel never married or had children of his own, living alone in his big modern eyesore of a house in our neighborhood of Dutch colonials and Tudors, always redecorating except for summers when Daniel came to visit and, finally, when Abel paid for him to transfer to college in New York. Daniel wanted to marry young, as both our parents had, though at nineteen I told him I wanted to wait, to know myself better, to build a life of my own before merging it with someone else's. But he'd insisted there was nothing I wanted to do on my own that we couldn't do together and that we were already practically family—Abel and my parents had adopted each other in exile and spent every holiday together. He believed that was enough. Eventually Daniel's parents started pressuring him to go back to Amman and leave me behind.

He didn't know my marrying him would not have been without controversy. My parents tolerated our premature romance because they'd known Daniel since he was a child. They understood and trusted Abel's influence; they could *all* keep an eye on us and chase him off if he ever became too much trouble. But my older brother, Santi, warned that if I married Daniel now or ever, our inherited culture, which hung by a second-generation thread, would fade to a more convenient English. Paternal heritage would dominate because Santi said patriarchy always wins, and I, as a daughter, needed to marry a full-blood Colombian like our father or at least an hijo de La Gran America, like us, with a foot in two lands, the product of our parents' great migratory experiment.

Santi held a practical policy on romance and wouldn't date a girl he wasn't willing to marry if she happened to become pregnant. I sometimes wished I could be that way. Especially when Abel told me Daniel was engaged to a Kuwaiti girl who'd been selected and endorsed by his parents because she came from a respectable Maronite family. Then I received a letter from Daniel saying he didn't really want to marry her even though she didn't have problematic ambitions like mine. He swore he'd love me into the next life. He swore we were *eternal*. I only wrote back, "Fuck your eternal," because I can be very mean when I make the effort, especially to people I love.

Maribel held her lighter to the hand-rolled tobacco stump on her lips.

"Don't worry, Lita. There's a collective amnesia that sets in after a few weeks in this city. If there *is* somebody, you'll forget him soon enough along with everything else that came before. How long are you here for anyway?"

"A year."

"Just one year?" Naomi was incredulous. "What's the point in coming if only for a year?"

"She can always change her mind," Dominique insisted. "That's what I did. And now I'm on my third with no plans of leaving."

"I've got to go back home in June," I said.

"It's easy to get a visa renewal. My father's got a good friend at the American embassy. Remind me to put you in touch, " Camila offered, as if that were the problem.

"It's the agreement I made with my family," I said, which left the others staring at me. "I have to go back."

I was grateful when Saira finally spoke.

"I'm going to Avenue Montaigne for some shopping this afternoon. Anyone want to join me?"

Giada and Dominique said they would. Tarentina took over, talking about her last trip to Marrakech with the Musician and how she'd run into a Swedish girl who lived in the House of Stars years earlier in the middle of Djemaa el Fna, turning the conversation into a string of anecdotes about their escapades, sketches of ways they'd uncovered their Paris together, making it clear that I was still as invisible as they wanted me to be, and there was a code to this house that was still beyond my grasp.

My classes at the language institute were full of expat wives who'd leave early for lunch dates, dilettantes on perennial student visas, and distracted businessmen who alternated between taunting and flirting with the young teacher. I soon started forgoing class for afternoon excursions with Loic, who was always ready to teach me something like that the Louvre was not only a great museum but also served as a popular destination for making out and express public screwing, as it had been for him and his friends as teenagers. He said they'd sip from flasks sewn into their denim jackets, get drunk in front of the Poussins or in the caryatid room, fondle each other between the Canovas, roll joints and smoke beside the *Sleeping Hermaphrodite*, and somehow never get caught.

It wasn't my first time at the Louvre. I'd navigated the galleries as part of a teen tour squadron when I'd won a scholarship to a summer language program: two weeks of Italian in Alberobello, two weeks of French in Fontainebleau, and two weeks of Spanish in Valencia, though when I returned home with a Castilian accent, my mother threatened to smack the conquerors' lisp out of me. But Loic taught me that if you wait until the late-afternoon tourist exodus, when they flood out of the museum into the dusty gravel of the Tuileries with exhausted enchantment, queuing up to buy Eiffel Tower miniatures from the Africans along the path, the museum staff is so worn from the masses that they'll wave you right in, past the security checkpoint, and won't even make you pay.

"Always go through the Richelieu or Sully wings, where the guards rarely check for tickets," Loic instructed as he led me through the great hall beneath the glass pyramid, "and if they do stop you, act as if it's your first time in a museum and you had no idea it wasn't free."

And he was right. We passed through without interruption, wandering up to the front salons of Sully where you can see through the Carrousel du Louvre across the labyrinths, past the Grand Palais down to La Défense on the horizon.

Later, when we emerged from the museum into the amber dusk, Loic stopped under the Carrousel arc to light a cigarette. I saw Gaspard walking a few meters away, recognizing him from the times we'd passed each other in the courtyard and he'd never offered more than a nod, always dressed in the same tired chocolate corduroy pants and black-and-white wingtip shoes. He was wispy in build like Loic with the same overbred floppy facial features, and though three years younger, he was terribly aged and wore a permanent old man's scowl.

"Look, there's your brother."

But Loic struggled to catch a flame with his lighter, and by the time he looked up Gaspard and his wingtips had already slipped into the hedges of the labyrinth.

He finally caught a burn on his cigarette and, when we were passing through the Porte des Lions corridor, asked, "Are you close with your brothers, Lita?"

"I'm close with both of them but they're not close to each other."

"Something about brothers." He drew in a mouthful of smoke.

I nodded, though in the case of mine, it was because there were ten years between them and I was right in the middle, five years younger than Santiago, five years older than little Beto.

"Where is your mother?" I asked. I'd been wondering.

"Los Angeles." He said it mockingly. *Loss Angeleez*.

"What's she doing there?"

"I don't know. A man, probably. Before Los Angeles it was Buenos Aires and, before that, Hong Kong. Always chasing men around the world, until they get tired of her and then she finds someone else. After our father died she had a breakdown. When she came out of the hospital my grandmother suggested she go visit an old friend in Rome to recuperate, but she met a man there and didn't come back until Théophile's funeral six years later."

"Do you ever see her?"

"The last time was four years ago. She was in Paris a week before she came by the house. I call her sometimes. She always says she has so many problems, so many pressures. 'Oh Loic, my life is so complicated,' but she never asks how I am. Never. She's waiting for my grandmother to die so she can claim her inheritance."

Loic threw the nub of his cigarette into the street as we stepped onto Quai Voltaire. "I feel worse for my grandmother than for myself or for my brother."

"Why is that?"

"Nobody deserves to be abandoned by their own child."

"Or by their own parents," I said, thinking of my own mother and father, but by the way he looked at me and nodded, I realized Loic thought I'd meant him.

We didn't speak the rest of the way home but I didn't mind. I've always thought sharing silence is how you really get to know someone.

Most of the girls had boyfriends, but in between romances, the girls had Romain. The maids called him Le Coq du Village. The girls called him The Corsican, holding him apart from the other waiters at Far Niente, the Italian restaurant on the corner of rue de Sèvres, who often stopped at our house for nightcaps after their shifts. Romain was a highly recommended bedmate, known as much for carrying high-grade hashish as for his Bambi lashes, that crown of gelled brown curls, a misty bronze complexion, and left cheek mole like the one Séraphine said she painted on in the forties.

I started joining the girls for dinner there, and on slow nights, Romain would stand at the edge of the table and share pieces of his life with me—how he came to Paris from Calvi by way of Marseille and was saving his sous to move to New York. He wanted to be an actor. "The French Daniel Day-Lewis," is how he put it.

"I want to study at Lee Strasberg like Newman and Pacino. I want to play all types of persons. Spanish, Russian, or Arab. I have the face for all these things," he said, touching his chin. "I don't want to be only a French actor. I want to be an actor of the *world*."

When he stepped away to tend to some other customers, Tarentina leaned across the table toward me.

"I've known him three years and never heard him speak so much, not even in bed, and that's where guys usually get around to spilling their dreams."

I shrugged. "I grew up with brothers. I'm used to hearing boys blab about themselves."

"I don't think he's looking at you in a sisterly way," Naomi said.

"I wasn't flirting with him." I must have sounded defensive because the other girls started laughing.

"On the contrary. You're a terrible flirt," Tarentina put me in my place.

"With no presence whatsoever," Camila added with squinty eyes and a thread-thin grin, as if judging me for a pageant.

Tarentina reached for the wine bottle at the center of the table, topping off my glass with what was left.

"That's precisely what is so brilliant about it, my dear Lita. Your charm is that you're charmless."

The other girls found this hilarious and I forced myself to join their laughter. I wanted them to think I had a sense of humor about myself.

"Romain was the first guy I slept with in Paris," Naomi said, suddenly nostalgic, and Maribel and Giada chimed in that he was their first in Paris, too, though only Naomi had ever been to the apartment in Gobelins he shared with a Polish housepainter.

I watched him across the restaurant as they went on comparing bed notes about Romain and the other waiters. The other customers had cleared out and the music was louder now. I saw a homeless man with a dragging leg in the doorway of the restaurant, careful not to step inside, waiting until Romain noticed him. Roman gave a smile and wave before slipping into the kitchen and returning with a wrapped plate of food for the man, who nodded appreciatively but never spoke before rushing off. It wasn't the first time I'd witnessed this ritual, though the other girls never seemed to notice, but that night I pointed it out to Dominique. She gave a quick look and said, "Oh, that's the mute who begs in the Babylone métro," before cutting back to the discussion of the waiters as lovers: Giancarlo, the stocky tanned one with the tiny hoop earring was in the lead for endurance, but Maribel had snooped through his wallet once and found a photo of a child he later admitted was the son he'd left behind along with a wife in Bonifacio. Franco, the blond from Verona, was Dominique's favorite, blond and frail like Loic. Lorenzo from Palermo was a tender and generous bedmate but all of them agreed that Romain was the best lover of them all.

Where I came from, mothers tell little kids that babies are freshly baked angels that fall from the sky and sex is meant to be personal and private like prayer. But Tarentina, especially, spoke of sex as openly as sport or philosophy, with proclamations that the greatest moment of the act isn't the orgasm but the five seconds before, and she wanted to live all her life that way, on the verge of being satisfied.

That night, the Far Niente guys came off their shift and joined the girls for a smoke and drinks in Giada's room. They called down to my room for me to join but I only got as far as the doorway, with Maribel rolling about on the floor, laughing with Dominique and waiting for her turn on the bong in Naomi's small hands. Tarentina was by the window gesticulating one of her wild monologues to Giuseppe the lanky Venetian. He pretended to listen, slowly slipping his hand into the butt pocket of her jeans, inching his pelvis closer to hers, and I thought if the girls had compared them as lovers, the boys had probably done the same.

Romain was stretched out on the floor, glossy eyed, blowing smoke rings to the ceiling. He motioned for me to come in but I shook my head and returned to my room to write a letter to my little brother.

A few moments later, Romain was tapping on my door frame.

"You have Tania's room," he said in English, looking around and then at the bed, as if he'd been there many times before.

"I know."

"She was more messy than you. And not as nice." He smiled big as if it were a much bigger compliment than it sounded.

"I heard she's getting married, in case you care."

"I don't, actually."

"Okay." I turned back to my letter.

"Oh, Lita. I frustrate, you know. I hear you speak English so easy and so nice and I frustrate. I want to speak like you. Tell me the truth. Is my English terrible?"

"Not at all." He had that French tick of tagging *uh* to every other word. "You just need to practice."

"But everybody I know speak more bad than me."

"Read to yourself out loud in English," I said. That was how my mother and I helped new arrivals and their children shed their accents. "It will help you loosen your tongue and feel the sounds on your lips."

"You make it sound sexy." He rubbed his neck against the door frame, catlike.

I shook my head, in case he was getting ideas.

"Why you say no when I don't yet ask you what I want to ask you?"

"No, your English is not terrible, Romain."

"I want to ask you to help me read like you say. I practice in front of you. You tell me when I do mistakes. Learn me words I don't understand."

He came close enough to take my hand as if he were asking me to dance.

"I pay you of course. Not a lot but I pay you something."

I thought of all the people back home I'd helped sound out letters until the words flew off their lips, how my own parents had once struggled with those foreign tones.

"I'll help you, Romain. And I'd do it for free."

He swiped a tattered copy of *Martin Eden* from the Lost & Found at the American Church, and a few days later we sat across each other on my bedroom floor as he read slowly but with an actor's precision, his brows like pointed arrows, features smooth and chiseled. I liked watching him. His thick thigh muscles creased through his jeans, bulging knees, square shoulders, perfectly erect posture under a tight ribbed sweater. He'd played in a soccer league in Corsica and even tried out for the professional clubs in Paris but wasn't good enough. He and his older brother came to Paris together, but his brother cried every night for three months until he finally went home to run the family butcher shop with their father.

"So you were meant to be a butcher," I said.

"In my other life, perhaps. It was the family business. I suppose I cheat my destiny by leaving home."

"Why did you stay here after your brother went back?"

He drew in his breath like it was a question he'd been avoiding for a long time and switched back to French, so I knew the words cost him.

"We had a happy family in Corsica. There was no need to dream of anything different. I only saw ten movies in my life before coming to Paris but when I arrived I met a girl who worked at the Gaumont and she let me watch movies all day without paying. That's when I knew I wanted to be an actor. I never had big dreams before leaving home. I discovered the longer I stayed away, the stronger my dreams became."

"Do you miss your family?"

"Of course. Love doesn't shrink as ambition grows. That's what I tell my parents when they cry that I've abandoned them. When I called them, my parents would always ask when I was coming home, so one day I told them to stop waiting for me because I will never come home again the way they want me to."

I thought of my father. He didn't want me to come to Paris. I'd heard him complain to my mother downstairs on many nights when I was supposed to be asleep.

"After all we struggled to make it in this country, and now she only wants to *leave?*"

My mother, my ally, lobbied on my behalf for six months. Wasn't this the very reason for their work and sacrifice, to give their children the opportunities they never had? Didn't he want me to have a global education and be a citizen of the world? Even though he seemed to accept my incurable longing for a broader life now, doubt lingered in his voice through every phone call home, a silent quandary only I could hear, his wondering why I insisted on elsewhere, why *home* wasn't enough.

"What about you, Lita? Why are you here and not one of your brothers?"

"I don't know."

It was hard to get Beto to even leave the house, and Santi loved his life so much, working for our father, dating girls we grew up with, and other than obligatory business trips, he barely ventured beyond a car ride away from home.

"It's the case in every family," Romain said. "There is the child who stays and there is the child who leaves."

Neither of us said anything for a bit. Through the thin walls we could hear Tarentina's stereo, the maids calling to each other on the ground floor below us, a pompier siren in the distance. He leaned back and reached deep into his pocket for his cigarettes, pulling out one for him and one for me. I took it in my lips and he lit mine with his silver Zippo, pushing my hair out of the way when it almost fell into the flame.

3

Séraphine said young women are most beautiful between the hours of seven and nine in the evening, freshly made up and perfumed with hope for the night ahead. She loved when the girls popped in to see her on their way to a soirée because she said it reminded her of her youth, and she'd have us pull photo albums from her armoires so she could show off the exquisite custom-made dresses she wore during Vichy times that made her irresistible to every man but her husband.

That night, all of us girls were expected at a party hosted by Florian Minos, a Greek-German painter who was also Maribel's teacher and recent lover. He was not married but living for twenty years with a Catalan dancer with her own flamenco revue in Pigalle. Florian was a local celebrity and his summer-end parties, legendary. Everyone knew him, including Séraphine, who first met him in the sixties when he was just a skinny art student in a fisherman's cap trying to crash her and Théophile's cocktail parties. Back then Florian made a living painting commissioned nudes for society ladies to gift their husbands or lovers, which was *the fashion*. He'd regularly bed his clients, too, which Séraphine said was an easy way to earn favors in this town.

The other girls finished primping, modeling potential outfits for one another in the hall along our bedrooms, short filmy dresses and shimmery heels as if still summering on the Riviera, while I went downstairs to visit with Séraphine. Some people are afraid of old people or just avoid them because they can remind one of death, but I loved them, maybe because I never had grandparents. When I was a kid, our neighbor Abel brought his mother from Amman to live with him, and I'd go over and have tea with her because I enjoyed her stories, even ones about her family surviving bombings and massacres, though I could never keep the invasions straight. She smelled like pistachios and my mother used to send Colombian food over, which made her gassy but I didn't care. Perla died in her sleep one night and Abel flew her body to be buried in Ramallah alongside her parents because that's what she always wanted.

Perla had worn tablecloth-looking dresses, shawls, and head-scarves, but Séraphine was always groomed, bejeweled, wearing one of her bed coats, and the maids changed the linens and duvet of her bed throne daily as if it were part of her wardrobe.

"Chérie." Séraphine put down the book she was reading when she saw me in her doorway. "You'd better hurry and get yourself ready or you'll be late for the party."

"I am ready." I was in my nicest blue jeans and a gauzy gray sweater.

"You don't have something a bit more festive to wear?"

"All my clothes are like this."

"That's impossible." I'd noticed French people love to say stuff is *impossible*.

She pointed me to the armoire, guiding me toward a tissue paper bundle on the top shelf. I brought it to her and she peeled back the layers, revealing a fuchsia kimono blouse with a black dragon painted across the back. She held it up with her fingertips.

"What do you think?"

I ran my finger over the delicate silk, as light as the tissue it had been wrapped in. "It's beautiful."

"It was made for me in Saigon. It's special but it shouldn't be a relic. Let's see it on you." She handed it to me and pointed me to the dressing screen in the corner of the room.

The blouse fit loosely no matter how tight I cinched the waist belt, and it cut low below my breastbone. I stepped out to show Séraphine.

"Pull your hair from your face, chérie."

I did and she seemed pleased, clapping her bony hands to-gether, asking me to spin for her several times.

"It suits you. You'll wear it tonight. But you mustn't tell the other girls where you got it, especially Tarentina. She's very jealous about these things."

"Thank you. I promise I'll take good care of it."

She pulled her cigarette case from her bedside table, took a stem for herself, and offered one to me despite the No Smoking rule she advertised to our parents. For decades she'd suffered from what she called a "butterfly heart," for the frequent fluttery sensation in her chest, a heart that skipped and reset itself. In her old age the leaps were wider, causing an occasional syncope, but she insisted that cigarettes calmed her heart better than pills.

Loic came through her doorway, his wet hair combed back without a part, wearing another variation on his gingham and trousers. Then Gaspard appeared and Séraphine's face brightened as if he'd fallen from heaven, the difference in how she looked at her two grandsons so evident that I truly pitied Loic, and I'm against pity in all forms.

Until then I'd only caught glimpses of Gaspard around the property or heard his piano-playing in the family wing echo through the house without regard for the hour. So, the piano was all I thought of to make conversation now that we were in the same room and Loic had made our first official introduction. I told Gaspard I thought he played Chopin beautifully. I should have stopped there but stammered that I loved Chopin and even though my father had never heard any classical music until emigrating, he said it was part of the human breath, proof that God exists, which is another one of those things that sounds much better in Spanish, forget about when I tried to translate it to French. My father had a hard time leaving God out of any conversation, always saying He was the head of his board of directors, which I don't think his accountants appreciated, but my father was a humble man with an excess of faith, and my mother wasn't too far off, equipping our house with saints on every nightstand, crucifixes over every bed, sewing scapulars into our clothes, a habit she picked up at the convent because it doesn't hurt to know you're covered should you die while you're in the middle of something.

Gaspard didn't smile. As far as I could tell, he didn't like people, so I was surprised to learn he would be coming to Florian's party, too. When I managed to shut myself up, Séraphine asked Loic and me to excuse her so she could speak to Gaspard privately, which I found strange, and when we were alone in the foyer Loic only said, "What can I tell you, Lita? There is always a favorite."

* * *

Six years earlier, a South African resident of the House of Stars disappeared from a group soirée and turned up without her shoes, wallet, and panties on the Cannes Croisette, with no idea how she got there. Loic took the train down to collect her, then, per her parents' request, put her on a flight home to Durban. As a result, Loic took his guardianship over our outings very seriously. We left for Florian's party en masse, squeezing two or three of us through each métro turnstile rotation, with Loic taking head counts. As we approached the party, he stopped to point out the golden torch on a concrete island within the traffic of Avenue de New York.

"That's where we'll meet if any of us lose sight of the group. You're not to leave the party without notifying me or one of the others," Loic said, meeting each of our eyes.

I asked Maribel about the torch because it looked important—a fat flame like the one in Lady Liberty's grip surrounded by a pod of tourists taking photos and posing by the mound of flowers at its base.

She pointed to the tunnel that ran beneath the torch's concrete landing.

"Down there is where the princess died."

We descended the steps from the sidewalk to a converted barge docked along the Seine between a pair of retired Bateaux-Mouches; a kaleidoscope of yellow paper lanterns and holiday lights, a band playing on the top deck as ladies in tiered ruffled flamenco dresses stomped, sang, and clicked castanets. Maribel was already half-drunk from shooting Tarentina's reserve Leblon cachaça with Giada and Naomi back at the house. She'd changed her outfit seven times before settling on a violet sheath that outlined her braless breasts and willowy frame courtesy of a dual addiction to Marlboro Reds and a spiced tomato puree her parents sent from Madrid by the crate. She'd already slept with Florian a dozen or so times, and Tarentina told her that should be enough to take the mystery away, but she was still nervous, even frightful, to see him. She gripped my hand as we crossed the drawbridge onto the boat. From her panic I expected a real stallion, but the guy who sliced through the crowd to meet us was older than my father, with a square head and patch of silver grass for hair, his skin lined and gray. He wore a batik sarong and a silk blouse that hung like a curtain around his protruding belly. When he saw Maribel, shy yet hungry eyed, he pulled her off my elbow and into his arms, bellowing, "Welcome to my kingdom," from behind her shoulder.

I'll never understand why people admire an exuberant personality when it's the kind I trust least of all, but the others were captivated by Florian's sultan persona, too, and quickly dissolved into the party.

New politics emerged on Florian's boat—the laws of the sea, I suppose. Until then I'd hardly ever seen Dominique and Loic speak to each other, but here they were holding hands, leaning into each other, Dominique's eyes doubling in circumference as she watched Loic point to something across the river. Giada described theirs as a long history of attraction, but Loic always halted before it went very far, so it was more like a long history of rejection, with Dominique offering up love like a paid vacation and Loic saying he'd rather stay home.

I edged about the crowd alone, spying my housemates throughout. Some of them saw me as I drifted through the tributaries of laughter and conversation but none waved me over to join them. Tarentina found her place by the bar among a group of male admirers, wandering from one end of the boat to the other for a change of view with the boys following faithfully like goslings. Giada hiked up her skirt and joined the dancing girls on the top deck. Naomi, without Rachid, who was training that night for an upcoming boxing match, defaulted to a cluster of American preppies from her school, and Camila hooked up with her crew of South American socials who didn't speak to anyone who hadn't grown up with body-guards and been driven to school in a bulletproof chauffeured car.

Saira and Stef found refuge in a quiet corner of the boat, talking into each other's eyes. They intrigued me the most. According to the BBC, Saira's father was about to be charged with war crimes, so you can imagine the guy knew a thing or two about intimidation, but that hadn't deterred Stef from being with Saira. She was tall, elegant, and fine boned with wide-set eyes and dark skin. He was a short, thick, red-haired, and peach-flushed native of Bruges with a port-wine stain like a handprint around his neck. I liked watching them together, witnessing the daily bread of their love, evenings spent watching stupid shows like *Starmania* or *Nulle Part Ailleurs* and cooking for each other in our dingy kitchen; that oasis state of certainty that the person you love loves you in return.

Maribel found me alone by the railing. I thought she'd come to keep me company, but it was just to tell me she was going with Florian to his bedroom on the deck below, even though his partner, Eliza, was on the deck across from us, twirling her arms along to the guitars of the Rasputin-looking leather-vested musicians.

"Keep it a secret," she smiled. "I'm only telling you in case I get murdered." A weird thing to say considering the deep crowd and murky water around us made the party on the barge an easy place to kill someone and get away with it.

* * *

I was one of the first off the boat when the police later arrived to break up the party, waiting for the others by the pile of wilting flowers and limp teddy bears at the foot of the golden torch.

A long-limbed guy dressed like a ninja graffitied the stone wall behind the torch with a fat black marker.

"Are you lost?" I heard someone say.

I thought it was the ninja, but when I turned I noticed the voice had come from someone standing on the other side of the flame. In the shadows I couldn't make out a face.

"I'm waiting for friends," I said with an eye on the tide of partygoers rising from the dock to the street. Loic and Dominique were among them, and behind them, Tarentina, who turned out to be old friends with the vandal, running straight into his arms squealing, "My darling Sharif Zaoui! Defacing Paris as usual!"

They chatted as the rest of us gathered. After checking in with Loic, some of the girls peeled off with late-night plans of their own, but the five of us left started on the long walk home with Loic. It was after two, the métro was closed, the Noctambus that stopped by the big nightclubs didn't pass this way, long lines had already formed by all the nearby taxi stands, and Saira had given her personal driver the night off on the one night we could have used his services.

We were halfway across Pont Alexandre when I realized Sharif and his companion who'd asked if I was lost were walking behind me with Tarentina. When he saw me look back, the friend pushed forward, and then, just as we came to the end of the bridge, he was beside me.

"Why are you following me?" A stupid question but I couldn't take it back.

"I'm not following you," he said, smiling. "We're going in the same direction."

He wasn't beautiful. People threw the word around like a rumor but I never did. It was a term more foreign to me than any other. My parents never referred to anyone as beautiful. When my classmates called me ugly, my mother told me beauty was an empty, made-up thing, but I knew it had to be worth something because Jesus and his army of saints always look like movie actors. I never understood the alchemy of allure or how some people get a reputation for being beautiful. My brother Santiago would say fantastically beautiful women never look as good the second time you see them, and a moderately pretty girl has the chance of growing more beautiful by the day. But I only came to understand beauty in school, through the principals of art dictated by scientists and masters like Da Vinci; symmetry, contours that capture light, balance and form—like the city of Paris itself, a perfect spiral of arrondissements, every park, bush, and tree lined and framed.

The boy walking next to me that night had none of those things going for him. One might say he was in the family of handsome, but askew, unkempt, with a marbled complexion like Paris fog, one green eye a bit larger than the other, one sideburn longer than the other, and brown hair that looked as if he'd cut it himself. There's nothing wrong with that, of course. My mother cut her own hair and ours, too, but his looked like it was cut while he was driving or frying eggs at the same time. His jeans and sweatshirt were too big for him, and with his hands thrust in his pockets he looked like he was carrying a weapon. He was as tall as I was, maybe an inch or two taller, but it was deducted by his slouch. His smile was misaligned. I could tell his teeth had never been fixed and thought of my own messy grin, twisted and concaved until shrouded in braces at eleven. Santi and I each wore them for years, and our parents, who'd been deprived of dentistry most of their lives, proud they could finally afford them, decided to fix their own neglected teeth, too.

Somewhere around Les Invalides, we stopped at a tiny flower box of a hotel so Naomi could beg the concierge to let her use the toilet. While we stood around on the sidewalk waiting for her, Tarentina declared that we should continue the party at the House of Stars and invited Sharif and his friend to join us. Sharif agreed on both their behalf.

It was late. There were few cars on the street. I didn't say a word and neither did Sharif's friend as we continued down boulevard Saint Germain toward the house, sometimes drifting one before the other, sometimes walking as a pair at an identical pace. I kept track.

Conversations in the House of Stars were a mishmash of dialects and linguistic collisions, flip-flops between French and Italian and Spanish, then to English to neutralize confusions, sometimes all in the same sentence. You'd think with so many of us speaking different languages there would be gaps in our communication, but it only expanded the banter. On the walk back from the party that night, Maribel revealed that Florian said that with her he'd felt a fléchazo, an arrow's shot to the heart, which did not translate directly, and the closest evocative alternate we came up with was *coup de foudre*, because *love at first sight* is long-winded and corny in comparison, and Tarentina theorized that monolingual English-speakers are thus long-winded and corny due to their verbal confinement because people can only experience emotions for which their language already has a name.

We convened in her bedroom with its own lounge area full of Moroccan pillows brought back from her frequent Marrakech holidays with the Musician, and ottomans surrounding a low table covered in liquor bottles and ashtrays. Sharif and Tarentina shared an ottoman and a joint while I kept to the edge of a lumpy purple sofa next to Maribel and Naomi. The couples—Loic and Dominique, and Saira and Stef—took to the floor.

Sharif's friend turned out to be his cousin, Cato, which Loic alerted "is not a French name."

"My given name is Felix."

"I think nicknames are a farce," Tarentina shot back with an eye on me. "A Danish guy once called me Tina and I rammed my mobile into his crotch for taking liberties."

She threw her head back with laughter, one of her moves for flirting with the whole room, and everyone else laughed, too. But I felt Cato's eyes fall my way.

Sharif said his father was Moroccan, which is why he had an Arab name, but his mother would call him Serge in public and within certain circles. Depending on the company, he'd play the part of the little French boy or the little Maghreb son.

"What does she call you now?" Naomi asked.

"She doesn't call me anything. She's dead."

Everyone fell quiet, so Sharif told us the story of his parents' meeting in "quintessential French form, at beach resort in Agadir." She was a twenty-two-year-old university student on holiday with friends and he was a guitarist on the entertainment staff. Some girls exchanged glances and let out nervous, confessional laughter.

"You see," Sharif mocked them. "It's a common story."

I looked to his Cato to see his reaction and saw his eyes were already on me, looking for mine.

The night ended around four. Those of us who remained left to our rooms, while Sharif pressed up to Tarentina in her doorway, but she pointed him out with a finger to his chest.

Cato waited for Sharif by the top of the stairs across from my room.

"It was nice to meet you," I said as I unlocked my door and stepped inside.

"Same to you."

I had an instinct the moment could be unfolded and pushed myself to say more.

"Do you live nearby?"

"No, I live on the coast, a few hours north, but I'm staying on rue Vaneau for now."

That wasn't more than two or three blocks away from Séraphine's.

"Are you on vacation?"

He shook his head. "I came for a funeral. This morning."

"Oh, I'm sorry." I felt like an idiot for asking.

"It's okay. It was my grandfather. He was one hundred and two. He was always complaining that he was bored with life. Nobody was as surprised as he was that he lived so long."

Sharif made his way down the hall toward us, giving a final glance back to Tarentina, but she had her boys she gave into and others she preferred to keep simmering. Cato's eyes didn't leave me as Sharif started down the stairs ahead of him. I waved good-bye and slowly closed the door between us but didn't step away until I heard their steps fade into the foyer below and the creaky house doors push open and lock shut behind them.

4

We might have all been greenblood progeny, but I had a very different relationship to money than the other girls, who went on daily shopping sprees on Faubourg Saint-Honoré, or rue Cambon, where some boutiques even closed so Saira and Dominique could shop privately. The girls always tore off the tags before coming home because, Tarentina warned me, the maids had a habit of stealing from every girl in the house but Saira, because they were afraid of her father. When I went into a shop alone, which was rare enough, the sales people ignored me or followed me around, and not because they were looking to make a sale. My housemates teased me, called me a stingy sous pincher, but I thought that kind of wild spending is learned at home, along with the dreamy faith that a new outfit can have the power to change a life.

Most of the other girls had never worked and didn't plan on a career beyond the task of marrying well, but I'd always had jobs, whether packing boxes or answering phones in my father's factory, bookkeeping for Raul the baker and Juanita the seamstress, or filing at Hector's law firm. Our parents never understood the American way of kids going to summer camp or just loafing around waiting to get into trouble, and were deeply afraid our cushy lives put us at risk for being useless to society. Papi insisted we weren't children of privilege but children of sacrifice. He said work made us honest, work made us human, and service was the rent we paid for the space we occupy on this planet.

My father's rule was always that the only free bed and free meal is at home. With my coming to Paris, he agreed to cover my rent, tuition, and food, but I'd have to work for anything extra. I imagined it would be easier to find work in Paris, but I quickly learned that the limitations on my student visa and the national deadlock on foreign workers made it impossible for me to find much paid work beyond under-the-table babysitting, housecleaning, or nude modeling like Giada did, though it earned her a thousand francs an hour. But Tarentina got me an audition as a candy-and-cigarette girl at a club owned by Gaetan, a former tennis pro turned nightlife impresario whom she dated her first year in Paris. I was supposed to roam the club strapped with a tray of smokes and lollipops, and I'd only earn tips, but at the last minute he assigned me to the coat check instead. I was expected to stay until closing at five in the morning, but the boss caught me dozing on the wooden stool in the corner sometime after three and told me I was not cut out for the nightlife after all.

I asked Romain if he could find something for me to do at Far Niente, but he said I'd have to be at least Corsican if not a thoroughbred Italian to work there because the owner was a bloodhound for legitimacy. At the end of one of our *Martin Eden* afternoons, he took me to check out job offers posted on the bulletin board at the American Church and together we combed the *FUSAC*, circling ads looking for English tutors. I called a few numbers but every single person, upon hearing I was American, said they wanted to learn from a Brit because they preferred the accent.

The one guy who did agree to interview me asked to meet me all the way in Porte de Montreuil. Romain and Loic both offered to accompany me but I decided to go alone, which in the end was a bad idea because the man, a white-haired Czech with a half-open pants zipper who seemed to speak English just fine, kept grabbing my thigh under the café table and saying smarmy stuff I was too embarrassed to repeat when I later reported to Romain.

The only income I'd made in Paris so far was the five hundred francs Dominique offered me to write her a paper on the Fauvists for her contemporary art class—a bargain for her because the Sorbonne PhD she usually paid to do her papers charged two thousand a pop.

Naomi's boyfriend, Rachid, assured me he could find me a job at the Puces market where he worked weekends. The other girls said they wouldn't be caught dead working at a flea market, except Naomi, who considered herself the most open-minded and democratic—the aspiring photojournalist who defied her Israeli parents by openly keeping an Arab lover, and who, before Rachid picked her up outside the Pompidou, had a brief affair with the young Senegali who sold fruits outside the rue du Bac métro and another with one of the Cuban defectors who got paid to dance by the song at a Latin disco on boulevard Saint-Michel. There was no point in coming all the way to France just to date another muted square like the boyfriend she had at home, she proclaimed, or worse, waste her time being faithful to him when she had the chance to try on other lives through the men she met here in Paris.

The morning after Florian's party, Naomi and I made our way through the sleepy streets of Saint Germain and boarded the métro to meet Rachid at work. After transferring at the Saint-Lazare station, I leaned into my plastic seat, and a newly familiar face came into view beyond the Plexiglas window.

It was Cato, standing across the tracks on the opposite plat-form still wearing last night's clothes.

I'd thought about him since waking up with the sunrise, touching the banister where he'd stood the night before as I de-scended to the dining room, taking my coffee alone while the rest of the house slowly rumbled awake.

I'd thought of him as Naomi and I walked the cobblestones of our desolate block glistening from the street cleaners' nightly rinse, picturing him hours earlier, making his way home after our shared night, not entirely sure how, since we'd only exchanged a few words, he had penetrated my consciousness.

And there he was.

"Look," I pointed him out to Naomi. "There's Cato from last night."

"Where?" She made a vague effort to look but was distracted by the old woman who'd boarded the train at Concorde and sat beside her, complaining in whispered English that she could smell her whole apartment down to the sardines and cornichons she'd probably left out on her kitchen counter.

"There," I said. I waved to him just as the train started vi-brating forward, and to my surprise he waved back before our train rattled down the track into the dark tunnels.

Naomi came to the Saint-Ouen flea market every Saturday, and the veteran vendors were used to the sight of the waifish American girl with the large camera hanging from her neck, with her pastiche French, hanging around the Egyptian boys. She led the way through the labyrinth of kiosks, barns, foldaway shops, the fortress of carpet shops, vendors of shoes, and leather goods, as streams of shoppers drifted through improvised aisles as if on a slow conveyor, behind every turn the start of another serpentine market row. Naomi told me about the boyfriend she left behind in New York, a boy she'd been with since tennis camp who expected to marry her upon graduation. I tried to see her as a young would-be bride, but only saw the Naomi she was now with Rachid, spending afternoons hanging around Les Halles, smoking his Gitanes, getting by on both ends of their broken Franglais.

She brought us to the booth where Rachid and his friends sold Rai CDs, hats, and T-shirts emblazoned with FREE PALESTINE, GAZA RESISTANCE, and ILLEGAL OCCUPATION slogans, with red, white, green, and black flags whipping in the wind overhead. She'd been photographing Rachid for as long as she knew him, with an entire wall in her bedroom dedicated to her *Rachid dans Paris* oeuvre; photographs of Rachid and his friends working at Les Puces; Rachid performing his hip-hop-argot poetry at smoky clubs and cafés in Saint-Denis and Aubervilliers; Rachid at the boxing club training for night fights on the amateur circuit, Naomi documenting the subsequent broken noses, missing teeth, and eyebrow tears.

"Lita!" Rachid grinned when he saw us. "I'm happy to say I've found you a job. A friend of mine needs a salesgirl at her antiques stall and she's agreed to try you out."

We followed him down the path to the barns and he explained that she was an older Ukrainian woman who needed someone trustworthy and I had an honest enough face, but after our introduction it took only a minute of small talk for the lady to start apologizing to Rachid that the arrangement would not work out.

"I can already tell she doesn't have the personality to sell a thing," she told him before turning to me. "I'm sorry. I can't afford to lose money on you."

"You could at least give me a chance," I said. "I'm a very hard worker."

She looked skeptical. "Have you ever sold anything before? Hand to hand?"

I considered lying, but my pause was proof enough and she shook her head emphatically as I sputtered, "I can learn. I can learn to do anything."

"Rachid," she was more clearly comfortable dealing with him than with me, "I need someone with experience. I know you understand. Explain it to her, yes?"

"She speaks five languages," Naomi came to my aid. "That has to count for something."

But the woman already had her eye on some potential customers fingering a small bronze statue of a lady petting a bear and waved her palm toward me indicating our meeting was over.

Rachid found us a table in a tearoom carved out into a tent between furniture stalls. Our waitress couldn't have been older than sixteen.

"Look at that," I said. "Why can't I get a job doing what she's doing?"

"My friend," Rachid dragged on his cigarette, "Don't take it personally. Les Puces, like Paris, runs on connections."

"It's kind of hard not to when they're blaming your personality."

"It's too bad you're not Arab. I'd hire you myself but nobody is going to buy a FREE GAZA shirt from a Colombian girl."

"She doesn't need to speak Arabic to take people's money and give them change," Naomi argued. "It's mostly tourists around here anyway."

"Look around us, girls." He motioned to the crowds swelling the flea market pathways, a mix of euphoric map-in-hand travelers, troupes of denim-clad teenagers, and hobby-haggling collectors.

"People don't come to the Puces for the merchandise. There is nothing in any of these stalls that anybody *needs*. People come for the experience of being sold to. They want conversation. They want smiles and charm. They want to feel like they've discovered a treasure, and they want a negotiating adventure as part of the show so when they take their little prize home and their friends ask, 'Where did you get that?' they have a passionate tale to tell. Nobody comes to the Puces for the junk we sell. They come here for the seduction. They come for the *story*."

"That's a long way to go for a story," Naomi said.

Rachid laughed at her. "Look at you two girls. You came all the way to Paris, for what?"

Naomi didn't hesitate. "To get away from home. A long vacation."

"I came for education," I said, though I didn't even believe it myself.

"Liars." He shook his head. "For a vacation, you go to Club Med. And, for education, you could have stayed home. Both of you came to Paris for the same reason all these people come to the Puces. You came for a story."

My mother hardly traveled except for her charity missions back to Colombia delivering medicines and clothes she'd spend all year collecting. She and my father weren't vacation types. If she were to go anywhere out of pure pleasure it wouldn't have been Paris but to Lourdes, on one of those all-inclusive religious pilgrimages. Though she'd long ago defected from her gang of nuns, she remained an aficionada of the divine and made me promise that I'd visit a church up the road from the House of Stars at least once. She'd heard it was a real miracle factory and wanted me to add to the chain of prayers for my brother Beto.

I didn't like to talk about him. I wasn't secretive but I'd read plenty of books on his condition, comparable case studies, and even took an additional minor in psychology hoping to understand him, though I'd never met another boy like my little brother, gloomy from the womb, never kicking, as if he didn't care whether or not he was born. I'm not exaggerating. I hate exaggerations. Life is unbelievable as it is.

She will never mention it, and I only know because I was five at the time and have been cursed with a very sharp memory: Beto's birth almost killed our mother. He never smiled, never laughed, and barely played as a toddler. Mami thought maybe he was disabled, but he walked fine and spent his energy wiggling out of hugs, running away from us. He was born on a hunger strike, too, and now, at fifteen, Beto was skinny like a girl before her period, with dim muscles and a curved spine, shadowy eyes and stringy veins pushing up through his temples. My father would warn you not to judge, say we're all crooked in some way, and I loved my little brother, but love isn't enough of a word in any language to describe what one feels for a sibling who can't stand to feel life around him—a boy who, as a seven-year-old, turned blue and fainted at the dinner table because he drank laundry detergent before we sat down to eat. A year later, he tried to drown himself in the bath, so our father had the tubs taken out of the house, the swimming pool drained, and the windows bolted shut, fearing Beto's entire existence was a suicide mission.

My mother said Beto's was an illness just like those of the sick kids in the orphanage she funded back in Leticia. Kids born missing limbs from contaminations, abandoned children with jungle diseases, born unwanted, which she said was the hardest malady to cure of all. Papi said when he was a kid he had every reason to want to curl up and die, but he heard the moon whisper to him at night that he had to wake up the next morning.

They didn't understand the monster eating their son, so they paid for every treatment available. Therapists, pills, art therapy, music therapy, sending him to a ranch for depressed kids, buying him whatever he wanted. Beto had a thing for rabbits just like Séraphine's husband, Théophile, had a thing for cats. Our house was full of animals—five dogs and seven cats, all former strays, a blind parrot and six rescued horses that roamed the corral we once used as a soccer field—but the only thing that kept Beto going was the bunnies he kept in the atrium, which used to be a greenhouse for Mami's tropical plants until Beto turned it into a free-range rabbit sanctuary because he didn't believe in cages. Our parents indulged him because that's what you do when you want to love someone into happiness.

I found the church easily because of all the beggars out on the sidewalk. Even though there was no Mass, the pews were packed, heads hung in prayer, the altar before the blue-cloaked virgin lined with kneelers. A long painted banner on the dome above the altar said that whatever you asked for here would come true, and that's probably why the place had such an impressive turnout. I got on my knees on my mother's behalf because I knew she'd kill to be here, and what kind of skeptic would I be if I didn't keep an open mind to prayer. Like my father says, the closest thing to faith is doubt.

Please keep my parents safe and healthy so they don't drop dead before I have a chance to make them proud of me. Bless Santi so he doesn't get anyone pregnant and stops drinking and driving. Bless Beto so he doesn't accidentally kill himself on purpose.

I didn't know what else to pray for. I'd been lucky all my life. So I prayed to be a better person. Productive. Useful. Not the kind of girl who just is.

And then I added one little selfish prayer, for love, which I thought could pass for an honorable pursuit, but it was an amorphous prayer, as if I didn't even know the words to my own wish.

I was hogging prime kneeling real estate with people waiting for a turn behind me, and my legs were stiff. I stood up and went to the gift shop to buy my mother a little silver medal of the virgin, which I figured she'd sew into Beto's pillow or something. She was sneaky like that; there was a time when the lady used to sew santos into my panties to protect me from taking them off for boys.

The three o'clock sun was still high, so I ducked into a small fenced park, a playground at the far end with children on the swings but they weren't the noisy kind, so I settled onto a vacant bench along the perimeter. I'd been walking around Paris with a stack of postcards since my arrival. My plan was to pre-stamp them, jot things down whenever I had a moment of inspiration, and drop them in a mailbox so Beto would receive a constant stream of correspondence and know I was thinking of him, because he was still refusing to speak to me whenever I called home.

When he was born, I decided Beto was my baby. I watched him in his crib, poked his fat cheeks, tickled his toes, and picked his outfits. My mother wore him around her chest like a scarf, and I envied her motherhood, the intuitive way she tended to his hunger, his burping, his changing. I pushed him in his stroller, held his hand as he learned to walk around the house. During his years of resisting solid food, sometimes he would only accept my spoon, and when he started climbing out of his toddler bed at night he'd come to me, not my parents, and curl into my side until morning, sleeping with a scowl, his fists clenched against his tiny chest. When his darkness overtook him, I was the only one who could get near him, and he'd tremble in my arms with the fear he was born with and stare back at me with the eyes of a beaten animal.

Beto didn't want me to come to Paris or to ever leave him. He was the reason I didn't live in a dorm when I went to college and why I chose a school nearby. The doctors said we shouldn't be manipulated by his threats, but I was a pushover. I spent years gathering the nerve to leave for Paris. Beto came to my room while I packed, moaning that I was the only one who understood him, the only one who looked at him without pity, who didn't judge him and think his life a waste just because he didn't know how to turn off the pain of living.

"If you really love me, you won't leave me."

I took him into my arms. I was the only one he let embrace him that way.

"You have to learn to live without me watching over you."

"You say that like you're not coming back."

"I'll always come back."

But it wasn't enough. I left him crying, and to punish me, he didn't come with the rest of our family to see me off at the airport.

There was a stone bust of a man on a pedestal a few feet away. I went to take a closer look and the plaque below indicated it was Chateaubriand—a helpful coincidence because one of Beto's rabbits was named Chateaubriand, and I decided it would be the subject of my postcard. Beto always gave his rabbits historical names. He was failing most of his classes but he was quite a reader, always stealing my books and scribbling *Beto Was Here* on the cover page when he was through. I wrote that Chateaubriand the bunny had a park in Paris named in his honor, described the iron fence, the manicured shrubs, the soft chatter of local children playing on the swings that sounded like the *Chapi Chapo* twins. I wrote that I missed him. I loved him. I promised I'd bring him presents when I came home for Christmas. Baby brother, cuídate.

And then I heard my name.

Cato's face came into focus across the gravel path. Somehow I'd walked through the iron gate without noticing him sitting on the bench opposite me. *How funny*, I thought, and then remembered to speak outside my own mind.

"How funny. I saw you just yesterday."

"No, the day before." He stood up and walked toward me.

"No, yesterday. At Gare Saint-Lazare. On the platform."

He looked confused.

"I saw you," I repeated. "You waved at me."

"I didn't leave the Seventh yesterday."

"Then it was somebody who looked a lot like you."

"Maybe you dreamed it," he smiled.

"No, it just means you're common-looking."

He walked closer. His shadow fell over me.

"What are you writing?"

"A postcard to my brother." I held up the image side of a Notre Dame gargoyle.

"Can I sit by you?"

I nodded and he sat beside me, only my handbag between us. I was never any good at chitchat, a hindrance to my purported goal of being a diplomat; stranger conversation was torture, even with a half stranger like Cato. I tried to think of something to say. Something intelligent and amiable to fill the air now that he'd made an effort to be near me.

"You don't say much, Lita. Are you shy?"

"Yes." No harm in honesty.

"Most people can't get enough of the sound of their own voice."

We looked at each other. It was strange to see him in daylight. His face, all sharp angles, pale sea-foam eyes flecked with bronze.

"My mother used to tell me the quiet ones have the most to say."

"Was she shy?"

"No, she said it to make me feel better. I was very shy as a child. I still am."

He pointed to the Missions Étrangères building beyond the brick wall at the far end of the park.

"She worked over there when she was young. Whenever we came to Paris she took me to visit her old friends there and then to play here in this park afterward. I always looked forward to it."

"You came to Paris often?"

"Not very often. Just a few times a year. My mother and I lived on the coast but my father always lived here."

"They're divorced?"

"No. They just preferred to live apart."

He went silent. My palms moistened and I slipped the post-cards into my bag before my sweat made the ink run, but he took it as a sign I was leaving and offered to walk me home. I immediately regretted having moved at all.

I wasn't planning on leaving but now felt I had to. He held the gate open and we stepped back onto rue du Bac. The house was less than a five-minute walk away but I walked slowly. I wanted to ask him what he'd do for the rest of the afternoon, if we could go back to the bench and sit there even if just to sit quietly and watch the children pump their legs higher and higher on the swings.

"How much longer will you be in town?" It was all I could manage.

"Not much longer."

We were already at the driveway. I thought I could invite him for a coffee or a cigarette like any of the other girls would do, but I only stood still, looking at my feet, then up at him, and he did the same. I could have asked him about his cousin. Anything to have a reason to stand there a moment longer, but he pulled back—no bise for me even though people around there were promiscuous with their double kisses—and gave a small wave just like the guy on the train platform he said was not him.

He walked backward in the middle of the tranquil road, facing me.

"Maybe we'll run into each other again."

"Maybe."

The sight of him, the distance growing between us, hurt me more than seemed reasonable. This wanting to be near him, the impulse to jump into a void. There's only one word for it in any language I know—the Spanish corazonada, a premonition, an awakening of the heart. A tightening. A fist closing around it.

5

It was Séraphine's idea to have a party on the first full moon of October. She allowed one grand fête per season. Anything more, she said, was just a plea for attention. There was a box of calling cards she kept locked away printed with *Les Filles de rue du Bac* in raised black ink that she pulled out expressly for these occasions, giving us each two dozen to offer our special guests. The idea was that nobody should be admitted to the party without one.

Loic gathered us around the dining room table and had us draw up tentative guest lists to avoid overlaps. Tarentina reigned as the VIP queen at nightclubs full of the highly moneyed and their hangers-on, while Giada's network consisted of hippie kids, techno-mongers, and art students from Oberkampf to the Bastille. Dominique ran with the Phoenicians, the Persians, and the petrolbloods. Camila's leg was the Latin culos de oro, fresas, hijos de papi—children of moguls, politicians—current, couped, overthrown—the exiled and the kidnapped, who mostly circulated in private house parties. Saira's contingency, beyond Stef, was the Swiss boarding-school alums, African junior royals, and import/export heirs with whom she regularly ditched class for four-hour lunches. Naomi's original crew consisted of the Americans, Australians, and Brits who held their own pub mixers, which allowed them to live an illusory Parisian life without learning a lick of French, though she'd mostly left them behind for her crowd of one: Rachid.

Everyone had their circles but, like me, Maribel didn't have friends outside the House of Stars. She rarely associated with the other students at Beaux-Arts, who she said were jealous of her being born into artistic fame. Her world was the workspace she'd been assigned in Florian's studio a few doors down from Delacroix's old house. I stopped by sometimes after my classes and found her sweaty and barefoot even on the coldest of fall days in that unheated building. Sometimes she stayed all night, *working,* she said, and only took naps on the mattress Florian kept pushed into a corner of his studio to "rest his bad back."

By the time Loic asked me who I wanted to invite, the guest list was already a hundred people deep.

"I don't know," I told him. That much was true. "I can't think of anyone." That was a lie.

I'd been hoping Sharif's name would come up on Tarentina's list, since we'd run into him a few nights earlier during the Stomy Bugsy show at Le Bataclan. He pushed against the mesh of sweaty bodies to greet Tarentina. In his face I saw bits of Cato, the same pronounced jaw, eyes that drooped at the outer corners into a tiny web of wrinkles. But the real Cato was nowhere in sight, and I thought of him, even after we left the club with a group of dread-locked surfers from Lacanau on their way to some big-wave surfing in the Mentawai Islands; a good-looking but banged-up group, all smiles and happy to share their Kashmiri hashish with the girls back at their hotel in République. Naomi and Rachid had split a taxi home with Saira, Stef, and Loic. I'd gone along with the leftovers and the surfers, figuring their company was better than no company.

If Tarentina were to invite Sharif, I imagined he'd bring his cousin along, but she hadn't mentioned him, so I did, at the end of the list-making, as if it were an afterthought, but Tarentina quickly dismissed the idea.

Every afternoon in the week since our Sunday meeting, I'd walked past Chateaubriand's park hoping to spot Cato on the same bench. I'd wandered up and down rue du Bac hoping to catch him doing the same. The only person who caught on to my stalking was Romain, who, after seeing me pass Far Niente's window a few times in one afternoon, came out to the sidewalk to ask if I'd lost something, maybe my mind. I made up a story about dropping my métro card, and he joined my charade of searching corner to corner for a while before going back in to set up the dinner tables.

I expanded my hunt to include rue Vaneau, hoping to see Cato step out of a doorway. I'd smile and say I'd gotten off at the bus stop at Les Invalides and was on my way home, which wasn't so far-fetched, and if he was the gullible type he might think it was fate, a coup de destin, but it never happened.

I want to say this without sounding foolish: In the nights since I first saw him by the torch, I'd felt a surprising hunger for him. I longed for a time we'd never spent together, memories we'd never made, conversations we'd never had, kisses we'd never shared. A strange future nostalgia.

My education turned out to be very equitable on the gray market of international study. The paper I wrote for Dominique earned her an A, word got out, and within days I had a list of academic orders from other girls in the house and their friends. I experienced a pause of guilt because cheating is immoral no matter how you slice it, even if France made it nearly impossible for me to make an honest franc and I wasn't even a sans papiers. But Loic insisted there was something to be learned in my fraud; manufacturing all those pages wasn't intellectual prostitution but my own personal atelier for learning the subject of *people*.

In trying to write as the girls would, I listened to the stories in their voices, beyond my early impressions and the basic biographical sketches we'd exchanged, listening and trying to push past their conversation patterns. The way Giada never contributed an original thought, only commenting on those already offered by others. How Dominique, following Loic around with the broken-down look of a circus elephant, was unable to look at a painting without thinking first of its monetary value. Tarentina saw nothing but herself in everything. I showed her the same painting and she launched into a story about her girlhood, the first time she felt a boy's tongue in her mouth as he pressed against her behind a row of trees at the tennis club.

I thought that after I'd written enough papers and saved some money, I might buy myself a new dress, but the night of the party, I wore the best old dress I had, a black cotton shift with short sleeves I'd worn only once before, for my college graduation. It was fitted to the body without compromising modesty, hitting below my knees. My mother had made it herself after I'd gone to the stores and couldn't find anything I liked. Her eyes weren't so good anymore, but she refused to wear glasses, and I'd watched her hunched over her sewing machine night after night after the rest of the family had gone to sleep, pushing the fabric along, the needle puncturing seams she'd realize were crooked, pulling them out with her teeth, only to start again. With the dress I wore the military boots I inherited at fourteen from my brother Santi, who'd bought them at an army surplus. I took them off only when forced into high heels or in the depths of summer when I traded them for sandals, even though my mother complained they made me look like a member of the FARC.

Like my mother, I never wore makeup or blow-dried my hair unless it was freezing outside, so I was dressed and ready long before the other girls, who crowded around the bathroom mirrors, taking turns on the one power outlet in the house that wouldn't combust under hair-dryer voltage.

Romain and the Far Niente guys were rolling up rugs, pushing furniture against the walls in the grand salon, arranging the bar, while one of Giada's DJ friends set up turntables and speakers. In the commotion, nobody but me noticed when the bell rang.

I opened the door to a redhead in a furry blue coat and mini-skirt, looking as if she'd walked a long way to get here.

"I'm here for Loic," she said, but if he'd been expecting her, he would have told her to use the side entrance to the family wing.

She wouldn't tell me her name, so I left her in the foyer and went through the narrow passageway under the stairs and banged on the wall until Loic opened the door, his shirt unbuttoned, damp hair uncombed.

Later he would tell me her name was Élodie. She was one of his Avenue Foch prostitute friends and came to ask Loic for money to pay the babysitter holding her infant daughter as collateral. But there in the foyer, she only met Loic with the look of a guilty child and stared at me, unwilling to offer a single word until I was gone.

"Lita, I was supposed to go to the pharmacy to get a medication for my grandmother before it closes. Can you go for me?"

"Of course," I said, because Loic wasn't one to ask for favors. He was one to do them without ever getting thanked.

It was a jacketless night, the last thread of Indian summer before the blue season of winter arrived to smother us. There were three pharmacies on our stretch of rue du Bac, but Loic told me it was the one on the corner of Varenne with the diet pill display in the window. There were a few other customers in the queue snaking along the wall. Mostly old folks and a young guy ahead of me looking to buy condoms. I thought of Ajax, my favorite encyclopedia of useless knowledge, who, during junior high sex ed class, informed the teacher that condoms were invented in Condom, France.

The guy ahead of me couldn't decide what brand he wanted, so the pharmacy lady told him the benefits of each préservatif while I swallowed my giggle.

Someone touched my arm with a chilly hand. I turned and saw Cato, his green eyes reflecting the fluorescent pharmacy lights.

"You scared me," I said, though I was delighted, and his hands, though icy, had rushed me with an unexpected heat.

"I'm sorry," he slipped his hands into his jeans pockets. "I just wanted to say hello."

It was my turn at the counter, so I handed the attendant the paper with Séraphine's prescription and waited while she went to collect it.

"I thought you'd left Paris by now."

"Soon." He was beside me now, lips parted as if wanting to say more, but he didn't.

"We're having a party at the house tonight," I tried to sound spontaneous. "You're welcome to come by. Bring your cousin and whomever else you want."

I pulled one of the cards I'd received for this purpose from my purse, though until now I hadn't managed to give away a single one.

"You'll need one of these to get in."

He held the card with his fingertips and looked it over, smiling.

"Thank you. But I don't really like parties."

"I understand." I tried to appear unaffected by his refusal, as if he were just some fool from the neighborhood I'd invited out of friendly manners or pity. It was Saturday night. He obviously had other plans. He was probably at the drugstore to buy condoms like the guy before me. I looked around to see if there was a girl waiting for him nearby, but his hands were empty, and there was no one.

"Thank you for inviting me," he said, tucking the card into his pocket.

"It's nothing."

My hurt turned to annoyance. He at least could have come up with a better excuse than not liking parties.

The pharmacist rang up the pills and I paid with the money Loic gave me. I mumbled a good-bye and started to leave, but Cato touched my arm again with his frosty fingers.

"Lita, wait . . . I'll come to your party. I'll see you there."

Séraphine wouldn't be leaving her room or receiving guests, yet she'd gone through the trouble of putting on fresh evening makeup, evening jewelry, an embroidered shawl across her shoulders, and a pair of jeweled barrettes in her white hair.

She looked lovely, and I told her so when I stopped in to deliver her medication. She locked her eyes on me for what felt like a full minute, and I wondered if I'd said something wrong.

"What's happened to you, chérie?"

"What do you mean?"

"You look quite different from when I last saw you. How shall I say this? It's as if your body is here, but you . . . you, my darling, are somewhere else."

I admitted I'd run into a boy I liked at the drugstore and given him one of those dumb cards for the party.

She became dreamy eyed, falling into a two-minute tale about some Guillaume she herself met at a pharmacy on rue la Boétie a thousand years ago, but he left for Indochina and never came back.

"Alas, we now have a more serious matter on our hands," she said shifting her attention back to me. "That dress you are wearing will no longer do now that the boy has seen you in it. It's now a dress you wear to pick up prescriptions. An errand outfit, not a party dress. You must change into something else. A dress of another color at the very least."

"This is my only dress."

"Your only dress? How can that be?"

"It just is."

"Very well then. We'll make due with what we have. Do you mind if we tinker with it a bit?"

I thought she meant adding a sash or a pin, but she rang her handbell to summon Violeta, her favorite maid, and when she appeared, Séraphine pointed to me as if I were a plumbing problem.

"Violeta, take this dress and raise the hem by one half meter. No less. And remove the sleeves. Be quick about it, please."

I ducked behind Séraphine's dressing screen and slipped off the dress. I tossed it over to Violeta and saw my initials where my mother had stitched them in turquoise thread in place of a label. A gush of homesickness came over me, remembering how I'd stood on the block of wood in my mother's sewing room while she measured me, humming one of her old Spanish songs.

Séraphine said to put on one of her silk robes hanging on the post behind the screen while I waited for my dress to be ready. I did and sat on the ottoman beside her bed. She handed me her silver cigarette case offering a Dunhill. She lit her own cigarette with a surprisingly quick and steady hand, squinting at me.

"Why do you wear those hideous boots, chérie?"

I hadn't taken them off with the removal of the dress.

"I like them."

"Aren't you worried people will think you can't afford better shoes?"

I shrugged. "Is that what they assume?"

"Just the other day one of the girls, don't ask me who because I won't tell you, said to me, 'I admire Lita's lack of vanity. She really doesn't care what people think of her,' and I said, 'On the contrary. Our Lita simply isn't aware. It's the difference between bravery and oblivion.'"

"You're saying I'm oblivious?"

"Of course not. You are a smart, smart girl. We all know this. But if anyone asks, you say your boots are Saint Laurent, yes?"

I nodded just to appease her, exhaling long across the room. I was getting good at smoking. Séraphine even commented that I looked like I'd been at it for years already.

"To think, all this time I thought you had something with the Corsican."

"Romain?"

"I'm told he visits you every day."

"We just read together. I'm helping him with his English."

"And this new boy? Where did you meet him?"

"The night of Florian's party." I left out that we'd met on the street while his cousin graffitied the Pont de l'Alma.

"He's French?"

"He seems to be. I don't know much about him."

"Just that you like him."

I nodded.

"This is good, chérie. Autumn is when smart girls do like the squirrels gathering nuts and find a lover to carry them through the winter."

I chuckled and she waited for me to regain my composure before continuing.

"You laugh, chérie, but you must trust this old woman. Without a winter lover, a girl risks falling into melancholy, and if a girl has too many melancholy winters, she falls out of practice for love and it's nearly impossible to recover. Remember, you can't make an omelet without cracking eggs."

I'd just nod when she started philosophizing. Sometimes people only want to be heard, and it's a beautiful thing to watch someone switch from casual conversation to revealing a particle of their interior. Séraphine was happiest when you let her dish out free advice or give her a reason to talk abut 1932, her pinnacle year of the whole century, when everything was still grand and glorious and every man wanted a chance to become her husband. At least that's how she sold her past. She had loads of lovers in the first twenty years of her marriage before she and Théophile gave up and started being faithful to each other. A lineup of men and a few women—it was the fashion—but Philippe and Jean-Michel were the valedictorians of her memoirs. Jean-Michel, the groundskeeper of the Biarritz house, which the family had to sell off in the seventies, and Philippe, her all-time-favorite amant, a Canadian banker she met at Harry's Bar while his wife was in the powder room. For twelve years Séraphine and Philippe would each tell their spouses they were going to Mont Blanc for three weeks of spa cure, which was true if you're one of those people who thinks of sex as medicinal.

"Now that I'm old, I can be honest," is how she began her special confessions. "Most of the time people do not manage to marry the one they truly love. My greatest regret is that I didn't have the courage to hold on to my Philippe when everyone and everything in my life told me to let him go."

She sighed as if the memory exhausted her.

"But in the end, chérie, there was nothing to be done. Women of my generation were raised to betray ourselves in ways your generation will never know."

Violeta returned with my deconstructed dress. I put on what was left of it and stepped out from behind the screen to show Séraphine, self-conscious with Violeta there because she and the other maids referred to us girls as "the little sluts" when they thought we were out of earshot. Still, they always left a tray of coffee and brioches for two at Tarentina's door the mornings after she had an overnight guest.

I thanked Violeta for working on my dress and she muttered something indecipherable back, handing me the mound of leftover fabric, all tears and scissor cuts now. I walked over to the full-length mirror in the corner of the room and stared at my bare arms and legs, trying not to think what my mother would say if she could see what I'd allowed to happen to her gift to me, a dress I would never get back.

"It's too shor—"

Séraphine held up her palm to silence me.

"It's perfect. One must break the shell to get the almond."

"I really don't feel comfortable."

"Chérie, you must remember that to be beautiful or fearless, you only have to believe it and others will believe it, too."

"I've never wanted to be beautiful."

"Everyone wants to be beautiful," she laughed but stopped herself when she realized I hadn't meant to be funny.

"Chérie, you are only beginning to know who you are. Taste this night in your new dress. You can return to being the girl you think you are tomorrow."

By ten o'clock, the crowd spilled onto the house's terrace, through the foyer, drinks held to chests, filling the salon. The other girls were deep into the party while I hung back on the top of the stairs waiting to catch Cato's arrival at our door. At midnight, I was still perched on the second-floor landing alone. Tarentina came upstairs for a fresh pack of her cigarettes, designer menthols she bought by the carton whenever she traveled.

"What are you doing up here? You look like you've been banished."

She sat down beside me and handed me a cigarette along with her preferred gold lighter, though she had a whole drawer full of them, mostly engraved gifts from men.

I took my time lighting it to avoid responding.

"Lita, I insist you explain your sad face and why you're sitting up here wrinkling your tiny dress."

I told her about Cato, how we'd seen each other at the park and tonight at the pharmacy.

"So that's why you wanted me to invite Sharif! Why didn't you just say so? I never invite guys I've already slept with to our parties. They start acting like boyfriends and I can't stand that. But I would have made an exception to get Cato here for you."

"It doesn't matter now. I invited him myself."

"That was your mistake. You shouldn't have invited him. You should have mentioned the party and *not* invited him. Men like to be tortured."

She slipped her arm around my back.

"You can't be so sincere. That sort of energy repels a man. I honestly don't know who started the rumor that you're smart. You have so much to learn. Luckily you have me to finish educating you."

"How is it downstairs?" I was tired of talking about myself.

"Not too bad. Giada corralled most of the messy drunks into the garden. They can piss and puke in the bushes out there and nobody notices. I heard from Camila that Maribel and Florian left together."

"No," I said and pointed to Maribel's closed bedroom door. They'd passed me on their way upstairs earlier.

"Ah, of course."

"How's Loic?"

"The usual. He and Dominique are the happy hosts of the party, behaving like a married couple. By morning they won't be speaking and Dominique will be in a depression until it all happens again the next time. You know those chaste affairs tend to be the most twisted."

With Tarentina, you weren't required to respond in order for her to have a full conversation.

"Years ago, when I moved into this house I had a crush on Loic. I thought he was so nice to me, showing me around Paris, the way he is now with you. He never made a pass at me, but I assumed he was the timid sort, so I decided to make it easy for him, took off all my clothes and called him to my room. And do you know what he did when he saw me on my bed waiting for him? He covered his eyes, told me to get dressed, and left me lying there naked. *Naked.* So I asked him what his problem was and he gave me his miserable, gloomy Loic eyes and said, 'You're too good for me, Tarentina.' I said, 'Don't give me that crap, Loic. We both know I'm not too good for anyone,' but he just walked away. I learned something that day, Lita. I learned all men hate themselves a little bit. Some cases are more severe than others, but each man has a discreet personal self-hatred, and once a girl understands that, it makes dealing with them much easier. Take my father, for example. You know he killed my mother, yes? I'm sure someone told you by now."

I nodded.

"He thought she was in love with somebody else and maybe she was, but so what? He shot her in the heart and held her as she was dying, cried all over her, and then wrote a stupid note about how he couldn't forgive himself and that's why he shot himself in the head. A woman would *never* do that. A woman would wash the blood from her hands, find a way to deny it, and get on with her life. But you see, men are born guilty. Women are built to forgive and love and forgive all over again. Men are built for war and because we live in mostly peaceful times, they just turn on themselves. My point is you have to learn to get through life without being sentimental about boys because they are never worth the trouble."

"I see."

"Let's be honest, Lita. Cato was kind of strange, wasn't he? He didn't speak at all that night, just sort of cowered in the corner. There was something primitive about him, like that feral boy they found running around the forest on all fours years ago. A scientist took him home and tried to make him normal, but he couldn't handle captivity, so they had to let him loose again."

"They did?"

"No, I made that up. I don't know what happened because nobody bothered to keep record. Even freaks become boring after you've gotten used to them."

She had me laughing so much that I didn't notice the door-bell rang or hear the first time Loic shouted my name through the foyer. Tarentina and I leaned forward to see down the curve of the banister. Standing beside Loic at the bottom of the stairs was Cato, searching the faces of the party, looking everywhere but up, for me.

He kissed me on each cheek. It was the first time.

"I like your dress," he told me.

I tried not to feel like a sham. I led him to the salon toward the bar. The room, thick with people and music. Romain watched us from behind the bar. He poured us each a glass of the pink punch I'd helped concoct earlier that afternoon. It was made of four or five different cheap rums from Monoprix, assorted juices, and a bag of sugar. Romain had warned us not to drink too much of it—the quality liquor was behind the bar for us residents and our special guests—but Cato took the glass he'd been served and I did, too, though I noticed, as we moved to the wall chatting with Saira and Stef, then Naomi and Rachid, he never took a sip. I didn't have that kind of restraint, and it seared my throat, but I was too caught up in my growing wonder about Cato. We were quiet, but between us I felt a conversation, taking in the vibrato of music, a Euro electro pop techno symphony, and the pressure of bodies in the salon around us, until it suddenly became too much for us. We both looked to the glass doors to the garden and then to each other. Cato reached for my elbow and led me as if he were the resident and I were the visitor, through the party crowd to the terrace, across the garden to the stone bench at the far end of the property.

We sat together, maybe too close, because he moved a few inches away, and I worried that maybe Tarentina was right about my repelling him, but then he touched the top of my hand with his fingertips, light and quick, and I stared down at my palm hoping he would do it again. My parents, raised without physical affection, laid it on their children heavily, sloppy with hugs, forever pulling us into their chests, kissing our heads, making a wet mess of our cheeks. But Cato's touch felt tantalizing and loaded with secrets I wanted for myself.

"I can't stay long."

There it was: He was already plotting his escape.

"You don't say much, Lita."

"I don't know what to say most of the time."

"Say anything. Say what you're thinking."

"Why do you have to leave?"

"I told you. I don't like parties." He looked toward the house. It was just as Théophile had described, lights like stars replacing those lost in the cloud-quilted sky.

"Which one is your room?"

I pointed to the window above Séraphine's drawn lace curtains. I'd left my desk light on, my journal open to a blank page.

"I have to leave, Lita."

"I know. You keep saying that."

"I have to leave, but I came tonight to ask you if we could spend some more time together before I go back home. Maybe tomorrow, if you're not busy."

"When you do leave Paris?"

"I should have left already."

"Is something waiting for you at home?" I said "something" but I really meant *somebody*.

"Just home." He stood up. "Can I come for you tomorrow around noon?"

I enjoyed his eyes on me waiting for my answer and the way they shone when I nodded.

"Will you see me to the door?" He reached out his hand until I gave him mine, holding my fingers lightly as we walked toward the house and sliced through the party. I went as far as the bottom of the front steps, fighting the impulse to follow him as he walked away into the falling fog.

6

We walked all over Saint Germain through the Luxembourg Gardens, down rue Mouffetard across the quai to Île Saint-Louis. We grazed each other's shoulders when pushing through pedestrian patches but otherwise we did not touch.

We only spoke of the things around us; the street people, like the violinist at Étienne Marcel with the python wrapped around his waist, the guy playing the accordion for money over a drugged cat and dog tucked into a wagon, made to look as if they were sleeping together outside the Printemps department store, or the break-dancers dressed like clowns by the Pompidou. We'd stopped for a coffee at Café Trésor and eavesdropped on an argument between two lovers. They held hands across the small table until he pulled his hand away. He told her he wanted to leave her but she didn't want to be left. We listened as she pleaded for reasons, and he finally admitted there was someone else, Ophélie, a girl they both knew. I thought she would cry, but she called him connard, stood up, and walked off. I was proud of her. I think we both were.

We walked without a destination, yet I felt something within me take root.

I grasped that I would love him.

To observers we likely appeared as talkative as barnacles, and only knew each other a few days, but this inkling, this awareness, felt as real to me as my sore feet when we stopped so I could sit on the ledge of a shop window and loosen my bootlaces.

We continued in the direction of Place de la Concorde. As we passed the old opera house I asked why we didn't just jump on the métro. It seemed easier.

"You don't see anything down there."

"You see *people*."

But Cato resisted. "I don't like the feeling of being underground."

We took the bus instead. A young couple sat across the aisle from us sucking on each other's lips. I tried to keep my eyes on the window, on the hordes of tourists swelling from the top of Rivoli to the wooded bottom of Les Champs and the standard clusters of Asian couples on those *Get Married in Paris* package tours posing for photos. He wanted to walk across the Pont Alexandre, his favorite bridge, and when we were halfway across it, he touched my arm.

"This is where we met."

"No, we met by the torch."

"No, the bridge. First I was behind you and then I was beside you. It was the first time you looked at me."

From his pocket he pulled a fat black marker like the one Sharif used that first night to write into the stone wall of the Pont de l'Alma. He leaned over the side of the bridge and reached for the golden chariot hanging above the river and used his sleeve to wipe a small patch of bronze that hadn't already been tagged with graffiti. He then wrote *Lita et Cato* on the statue and looked to me with a slow smile.

"So when you cross this bridge you'll remember you were once here with me."

I thought this would be a great moment for a kiss, but it didn't happen. We grinned at each other, thunder stirring overhead, and got on our way again.

We were slow, though, and the rain fell fast. Within minutes we were wet, our clothes soupy, rain dripping off our lips and nostrils. We took shelter in the doorways along the quai and finally made it to the House of Stars as the winds picked up. I dropped to the foyer floor, peeling off my boots and waterlogged socks while Cato slipped off his sweatshirt, slim and shivery in his T-shirt, revealing pointy shoulders and a sloped spine. I hadn't expected him to walk me all the way home, but here he was and I hadn't yet figured out what to do with him. It was a big house, perfect for parties, but when entertaining just one person, the only place to go, it seemed, was the bedroom.

Séraphine heard us come in and called for me to come to her room. I left him in the foyer and found her in bed, an extra crochet blanket pulled around her shoulders, bifocals on the tip of her nose, and some dusty old book in her lap.

"You fell in the Seine, chérie?"

"The rain caught us." I pulled my hair off my neck and twisted it into a knot.

"You and the boy?"

"He's in the foyer."

"Bring him in."

I stole a few seconds in the shadows of the corridor, watching him look out to the courtyard as rain rattled the windows. He was beautiful. I understood it when I saw him then, netted in the white and blue glow of the afternoon rain.

"Séraphine wants to meet you."

I'd told him about her, but not enough to prepare him for the sight of alabaster Séraphine in her antiquarium, reclined like a sphinx. I introduced her the formal way, as Countess, which I think she appreciated. She offered us each a cigarette from her engraved silver case, an especially kind gesture on her part because she kept a separate box of Dunhills for guests and only offered smokes from her personal stash to her favorite people.

I accepted one, but Cato declined.

"You don't smoke?"

"No, madame. Never."

Séraphine was immediately suspicious.

"What sort of a name is Cato?"

"A nickname my mother gave me. I've been called that way all my life, madame."

"What is your birth name?"

"Felix."

"Just Felix?"

"Felix Paul."

"Felix Paul what?"

"Felix Paul de Manou, madame."

I slid my unlit cigarette back into Séraphine's case and stepped back from her bed to the wall, wondering if it was odd that I hadn't thought to ask his last name and he hadn't asked mine.

She noticed my retreat, moving her eyes to Cato, to me, to Cato.

"De Manou is not a common name."

"No, madame. It isn't."

"It's quite an unusual name, in fact. Is it not?"

"Yes, madame."

"Are you something of . . ." She paused, cleared her throat, and began again: "Are you something of . . . of . . . Antoine de Manou?"

"Yes, madame."

"He is your . . ."

She waited but he said nothing.

"He is your . . . great-uncle?"

"No, madame."

"No?"

"No."

"What is he to you then?"

I became annoyed. She never went through this kind of trouble with any of the other guys who came to the house.

"He is my father."

Séraphine's eyes went so big they looked taxidermied.

"Your father? That's impossible."

I think she expected him to try to convince her otherwise, but he just stood, quietly waiting for whatever came next.

"How old are you, Felix?"

"Twenty-two."

"You are the son?"

"Yes, madame."

"Are you aware the rumor is that you are dead?"

I thought that was a rude thing to say no matter what she'd heard but kept quiet.

"As you see, madame, I am not."

"But your mother?"

"Yes, my mother is dead."

"But not from the bomb."

"No. A car accident."

"Ah, yes, I remember." It was all coming back to her. "She took you away . . ."

"She took me to Normandy, madame. She never liked Paris. It was better for us."

"Is your father still in the Vaneau house?"

"Yes, madame."

"You never returned to live with him?"

"I prefer the countryside, madame."

She eyed him. "It must be peaceful. My own doctor often tells me a move to the coast will improve my health. Better quality of air, good for the lungs. What do you think?"

"A fine recommendation, madame, though you have a lovely home here."

In two minutes, Séraphine had learned more about Cato than I had in six hours of gentle meandering through Paris's passages. I thought you should let a person tell what they want to tell. When you turn on the questions it gives them the right to do the same to you, and I hated when people asked me about myself—always left with the feeling that no matter what I revealed it was either too much or not enough. That's why I decided to end the inter-rogation right then and there and told Séraphine we'd let her get back to her reading.

Cato told her it was lovely to meet her. I started for the door and motioned for Cato to follow, but Séraphine called after our backs.

"Felix, please tell your father that Séraphine de la Roque sends her regards."

Back in the foyer, he pulled his sweatshirt off the coatrack and threw his arms into the wet fabric. I didn't want him to leave but I wasn't ready for him to stay. In my bare feet he was two inches or so taller than me. We stood by the door and made plans to meet the next afternoon. He didn't kiss me, not even a good-bye bise, so of course, it was all I could think about as I watched him cross the courtyard in the rain hoping he'd look back at the House of Stars, but he didn't.

I couldn't stop Séraphine from spilling to me as soon as Cato was gone: how she'd known Antoine de Manou in the fifties when he was just back from Suez. Then he went to Algeria and she didn't see him for many years. He was always a jackal, she said, but now he was an old jackal with money and experience and influence, all of life's most dangerous things. He was on the Parliament until they grew tired of his radical antics. Now he was on the Assembly and had his own political party with the main objective of putting walls around the country to keep out *my* kind. I thought Séraphine meant Americans, but she hooted, "That's part of your problem, chérie. You don't even know what you are. But it doesn't matter your nation or whether you are a street cleaner or a greenblood, because Antoine de Manou hates all foreigners indiscriminately. He's the worst of France, chérie. The worst. No wonder that boy never mentioned him."

She told me Antoine's apartment was bombed when Felix was a baby. It might have been the Basques, Algerians, or Corsicans. It was never decided because so many people hated him. Except his small yet devoted following. Even the devil, Séraphine said, has fans.

"If he has an ounce of his father's blood, you should be very careful, Leticia."

I told Séraphine that Cato was different. The only French thing I could point to about him was his language.

"And yet that's everything."

"Maybe in your generation. Not in mine."

"Chérie, a wise man once said racists, misers, and saints are always the last to be aware of their condition."

"What wise man?"

"My Théophile. He was very wise sometimes."

"I don't think it matters who his father is."

"Of course you don't. *Your* father is the Colombian Oliver Twist." She laughed, and I sensed that it wasn't the first time she'd spoken of my family that way. "You don't understand lineage and bloodlines and why these things matter. I am starting to think it might be too late for you, Leticia. You might never catch on."

"We can't choose our fathers just like we can't choose our children."

Though I'd been offended, I regretted my words instantly.

"I'm sorry," I said but somehow my apology didn't translate, and Séraphine stared at me, shaking her head slowly.

"You are very young, Leticia. Life has a way of humbling the arrogant. And I am reminded that I am an old, old woman when I look at your face and know that you will not listen to a word I have said."

I thought of my parents, the moment my mother said she knew she would spend her life with my father. She saw him from her window in the convent. It was an overcast Bogotá day, and he worked on that fence for hours before stopping to eat under a tree on the edge of the convent garden. She couldn't make out his face, but she said she might as well have been blindfolded, because the feeling had come to her even before he arrived that morning, the knowledge that he was whom she'd been waiting for. They didn't speak until many weeks later when his work on the fence was nearly completed and she'd gone out to the garden to bring him a piece of cake left over from a birthday celebration for one of the nuns. To hear it from my father is to hear a recipe, a poem he spoke to the sky every night that he slept in the bed made of old car seats in a corner of his boss's garage. He'd asked for a woman adrift like him, a woman with whom he could start a family, craft a dream, a woman within whom he could find his purpose, and himself.

My brother and I used to laugh at our parents' old-world love story. We understood how they'd found refuge in each other, but I think we thought ourselves better than to naively surrender to a divine providence. With our American privilege had come a certain sterility and cynicism that I was surprisingly pleased to now be shedding. It was as if my blood had been moving slowly through me for years, and with Cato my pulse had been altered, changing course. No matter what I was told about the family name that preceded him, I knew I'd found a new piece of my life in Cato, stepping into my fate as if claiming a part of my inheritance.

7

I'd already been to the Rodin Museum with Loic. Cato didn't want to go inside the museum, only toward the back garden, through the pebbled pathways along the tree-lined perimeter, around the fountain to the sphere of benches dappled with tired travelers and local lovers resting their heads in each other's laps. He stopped to buy a sandwich from the café by the hedge and we settled onto a vacant bench at the far end of the museum grounds.

He offered me half of the sandwich and I took it.

"I'm leaving tomorrow, Lita. I have to go home."

"Do you have a job waiting for you?"

"Yes, but that's not why I need to go back."

"A girlfriend?"

"No."

"What then?"

"I love being with you."

The word *love* from his lips, vertiginous.

"But . . ."

"But what?"

"I can't stand Paris." His face was suddenly shadowed. "This city makes me ill."

"What do you mean?"

"Every day that I'm here I search for the horizon and I can never find it through the buildings. I look for earth but there's only concrete. I can't get the noise out of my ears. And the air. Can't you feel how heavy it is?"

I inhaled deeply. Cool, dry air, the fall fragrance of leaves and ash.

"It's just *air*."

"It's suffocating. I feel starved for real air here, and like a zombie among a million other miserable faces."

He stared at me gravely, almost as if I were to blame.

"I'm not made for the city. I need ocean air. The open sky. I need friendly faces. I wish you could see where I live. Then you would know what I mean."

I felt the warm October sun on our faces. The noise was the song of a city, conscious, pulsating. Some days we'd hear about the pollution levels going up, only half the cars could drive, and the government recommended staying indoors, and as for misery, in my month in France I'd seen three or four strikes—the Basques, the university students, and the taxi drivers. But all these things are proof of life, a society, a civilization.

"Every place has its flaws," I said. "I love Paris for what it is, not for what it isn't."

"I'm trying to tell you I can't stay here another day."

"When are you leaving?"

"Tomorrow morning on the seven o'clock train."

"You've already booked a ticket?"

He nodded and we looked at each other but didn't say anything more.

I care too much. I can't help it. It's congenital. I care too much about life, particularly about people. Santi would say it's the immigrant genes; immigrants are genetically predisposed to caring about life too much, which is why they put themselves in all sorts of crappy circumstances hoping for a better tomorrow. That kind of hope is a disease. If you carry the chromosome for faith you're doubly terminal because you'll always believe your misfortune is a prelude to something better.

So he was leaving.

I chewed the last bits of my sandwich with my best je m'en fous face. Cato watched me, but I watched the fountain, the silver water spots of coin-tossed wishes. I made a silent penniless wish that he would change his mind and thought he might have when he touched my sleeve gently, but it was only to say, "I'll walk you home."

"You don't have to."

He looked puzzled and I was pleased. He deserved to be confused.

"You seem upset, Lita."

"Why would I be upset?"

"Because I'm leaving."

"You've got to go back to your life. Besides, we hardly know each other." Loic the nonpracticing actor would have been impressed with my delivery.

I stood up and took a few steps toward the fountain before turning back around to him, inhaling as if I couldn't get enough of this alleged putrid air around us.

"Thank you for a *lovely* afternoon."

I'd already charted the scene, expected him to come after me. But by the time I crossed rue Barbet de Jouy, hot in the face, I realized Cato had no plans to follow.

My parents have always prided themselves on their manners, which is funny considering they were both raised like wildflowers.

The nuns taught my mother to be quiet, acquiescent, prudent, but those qualities are different than the manners that serve you at a dinner table or party. My mother learned hers from a Park Avenue lady whose apartment she cleaned during the early days of her and Papi's arrival. The lady was a grouch but grew fond of my mother because Mami spoiled Byron, her cranky Persian cat, cooking him filet mignon just the way the lady wanted. After teaching her how to serve lunch, the old lady would invite my mother to join her at the table for lessons on posture and how to hold utensils. Santiago and Beto hated hearing about our mother's days as a janitor and maid no matter how much our parents insisted there was no shame in honest work. When the Park Avenue lady died some years later, a lawyer tracked us down in New Jersey and said she'd left Byron to our mother in her will. We thought he was on his last legs but Byron got a second wind of life with us and lived for another ten years, though Santiago changed his name to Boyacá.

I passed for a lady most of the time, which pleased my parents, but our father also taught us to defend ourselves in case we ever got jumped like he did during his years on the streets. He took special interest in my self-protection because my parents believed that many men were rapists-in-waiting. He made us practice throwing and blocking punches in our home gym, taking my hands in his: "These hands look delicate, mi amor, but they are not. These hands are machetes."

Then he'd bring in one of the gardeners or handymen or whoever was around, instructing them to pretend to try to kill me to see if I could stop them. One by one they'd go for my throat and I'd duck, throwing my fist into their chests with all my weight behind it, and that is how Isidro the electrician ended up with a broken rib.

It's not like Papi was training us to be paramilitants or anything. We were pacifists, and I never had the chance to use my
violence until I was fourteen and won a state award for English
and some remedial girls started calling me a dirty wetback whore,
saying they were going to have my family deported, pulling my hair
and spitting on me as I walked through the school halls. One day
they followed me out to the parking lot. My body took hits, but I
blocked the shots to my face so there would be no evidence and
I wouldn't have to tell my parents what happened. They thought
their kids would be safe growing up in the suburbs. I didn't want
to be responsible for them losing their innocent view of my world.

When I left Cato that day in the Rodin Museum gardens,
the memory that came to me was of years spent training to fight
on a punching bag, only to emerge beaten and defeated, nursing
my bruises alone.

When I got back to the house, Loic was perched on the front
steps as he often was, waiting for someone, anyone.

"Why are you crying?"

"I'm not crying," I rubbed my eyes. "It's the pollution."

I sat next to him sucking on a cigarette like a pacifier, the last
scraps of afternoon sun tucking away into an early evening chill,
confessing everything.

"Forget him," Loic advised. "You'll find someone else. A local,
not some country mouse.

Tarentina later tried to console me by saying Cato had probably
been interested in me only because French boys think dark girls give
spectacular blowjobs, and when I didn't produce he decided to move
on. A few of us lounged in her room waiting out the afternoon rain
with cigarettes and coffee the maids had brought up with cookies on
a silver tray. Tarentina was stretched belly-down on her bed talking

about how she could write a book on the sexual tastes of European men—not a memoir but a manual filled with anecdotes from her years of fieldwork.

"Why don't you then?" I asked her.

"What for? Nobody reads books anymore."

But Naomi countered that Rachid and his friends said the paler the girl, the looser the panties.

"That's because everyone knows gringas are easy," Camila sneered.

"There is no easier girl to get into bed than an upper-class Italian," Dominique argued, and I thought Giada might take offense, but she instead offered that it was common knowledge that the girls most liberal with their bodies are the ones from current or former Communist regimes.

"You see, Lita," Tarentina explained, as if I were the last to know, "there are two types of lovers in Paris: the incurable romantics on the quest for love and those in pursuit of the exotic fuck. The problem is when these two objectives collide, as they seem to have done in your case. Am I right, girls?"

She looked to the others, who nodded in agreement and back at me.

"All that cross-cultural dabbling is fine for a casual affair. But in matters of love, the wise ones know it's best to stick to your own kind."

"That sounds kind of narrow-minded."

"Perhaps, but it's true. Count your blessings, darling, that he didn't stick around long enough for you to form any real attachment."

I felt all their eyes on me.

"For the love of God," Tarentina howled, "you saw him three times in your life!"

"Four," I corrected.

She rolled her eyes, groaning, "Of all the pretty boys in Paris, you had to set your sights on de Manou Junior. That is some incredibly bad luck."

I had no idea they already knew about Cato's father, but I learned you couldn't stop gossip in that house.

"I don't know what you mean," I said, but from the way Tarentina stared back at me it was clear Séraphine must have recounted every word of our conversation.

"Let me just say what everyone in this room already knows, Lita. He could never be with you in any meaningful way and it's obvious that's the only way you want it."

"He'd be laughed out of France," Camila added with an octave of pleasure. "He's probably already got a girlfriend anyway. A de La Rochefoucauld type."

"I'm sure he'd be up for a fling," Giada said, trying to sound supportive. "But you'd have to know it's like buying a pair of shoes, taking them home, and realizing they're just not you."

"I'm supposed to be the pair of shoes?"

"It's not *you*, Lita," Tarentina tried more gently. "You just couldn't have found anyone more terminally French than the son of Antoine de Manou, and you couldn't be any more of a foreigner. What you need now is an interim lover to keep you limber until you find your next affair. Why don't you try Romain? He's always hanging around you with that reading nonsense. And he comes highly recommended."

She and the other girls traded knowing smiles.

"Has he ever made a pass at you?" Camila asked me.

I admitted he hadn't. But as much as I enjoyed the sight of Romain and his lean cross-legged thighs on my carpet, reciting

Jack London, he hadn't captured my imagination. The one who lingered in my subconscious before I fell asleep at night was Cato, the picture of his silhouette walking through the dark rain, watching me from across an otherwise desolate street.

"Oh, girls," Tarentina sighed, "we've obviously lost this one already."

I was relieved they'd stop bullying me with their wisdom, but Tarentina offered one last thought.

"There should be a sign hanging over the front door of this house for every girl to see the moment she arrives."

"Saying what?"

"It's not love, it's just Paris."

Maribel was often depressed due to Florian's unwillingness to leave Eliza. She'd spend a string of nights at the studio followed by a week as a bedbound slug with Florent Pagny's *Savoir Aimer* playing on repeat in her CD player, until Florian appeared at the House of Stars pleading through her closed door and she'd finally let him in. I'd hear them through the thin wall that separated our bedrooms, the sound of weight shifting on her metal bed frame, the headboard slamming against the plaster wall, the sound of promises—his telling her he loved her and her inevitable desperate questioning growing louder and louder, "Then why won't you leave her?"

That week he had a new policy of non-response. Tarentina said it was meant to keep her hopeful, and hope needs very little fuel. She called Maribel an idiot for making demands. She said only the stupidest women think an affair can exist anywhere outside the bedroom. She'd been with the Musician for years already, and his wife had yet to catch on. He wasn't the only married man on her roster, either, but Tarentina was as discreet as a tomb, and her men knew this, which always kept them coming back.

"To be a successful mistress," she advised, "a girl must remember the relationship comes without ownership. Love and jealousy are symptoms that the affair has expired and it's time to gather your things and walk away."

She compared an affair to one of Maribel's paintings, saying no matter how obsessed she became with a piece, there always came a day when she'd look at it and know it was finished; not one more brushstroke could make it any better.

Maribel took medication for her frequent spiraling emotional states and, per her doctor's recommendation, long walks through the Latin Quarter that were meant to clear her mind. Lately, I was the only one willing to join her. That day, we started out at Café Mabillon and were chatted up by some Swedish tourists at the next table over. They mistook us for natives, and we flexed our Parisian accents and affectations, thrilled that they couldn't tell the difference. They were on their honeymoon, and I envied the way they checked each other's eyes after every sentence and spoke in a dialect of We. They could be mistaken for siblings and told us they were both accountants and met while working at the same firm. They paused to look at each other, and in that instant I imagined them in bed, the man's strawberry blond hair on the pillow, her feathery tresses against his chest.

We left them to go browse the stalls of the bouquinistes, and while Maribel checked out the book bins looking for interesting cover artwork, I eavesdropped on a brown-bearded American expat in a navy fisherman's sweater at the next stall over as he told a pair of Mexican backpackers, in French-spattered English, how he'd come to Paris twenty-five years earlier as a philosophy student but had fallen in love with both a woman and the city and never returned home. Now he operated a stall selling Belle Époque postcards and painting reproductions, but he was really a raconteur, a storyteller, a lover of words and the language of the soul.

I thought of my father. Once, before my graduation, I'd mentioned the possibility of changing direction and not studying diplomacy as I'd been planning. Papi thought I meant I'd join him and Santi at the family business, but when I said I was considering something more creative, he shook his head as if I'd been terribly mistaken and said there was no need for that; I was already an artist by blood; all immigrants are artists because they create a life, a future, from nothing but a dream. The immigrant's life is art in its purest form. That's why God has special sympathy for immigrants, because Diosito was the first artist, and Jesus, un pobre desplazado.

"It's not the same, Papi," I'd tried, but he shook his head.

"Pero of course it is, mijita. All your life is a work of art. A painting is not a painting but the way you live each day. A song is not a song but the words you share with the people you love. A book is not a book but the choices you make every day trying to be a decent person."

When we were on our way again Maribel looked to the American and sighed, "A thousand idiots come to Paris every day thinking they're artists but hardly any really have it in them. Look at me. I was born and bred for this shit and *I* don't even have it in me."

"Come on, Maribel. Everybody knows you're talented," I said, and it was true, but everyone also knew that Maribel was a third-generation painter of commercially viable lineage, with a greater chance of making money from it than the majority of her peers.

"Basta, Lita. I know what I am. I'm a great imitator. I'm learned, not original. But people can't tell the difference."

She talked as we crossed through Saint Germain, and seared through cigarette after cigarette, rambling that she wanted to disappear, dissolve into the earth like spit. By the time we reached rue du Cherche-Midi, she'd worked herself into a disquieted frenzy, stopping along the wall of a building to gather forces for the rest of the walk home.

A green BMW pulled up along the curb in front of us. Its windows rolled down, and a man in one of those checked shirts with the initials sewn into the pocket that Loic owned by the dozen leaned across the passenger seat and waved us over. I thought he was asking for directions, so I stepped forward.

"I'm looking for something tropical," he said.

I assumed "Tropicale" was the name of a bar or restaurant in the area and said I hadn't heard of it, but he laughed and pointed to Maribel on the wall behind me.

"How much for both of you?"

He could have been a father, a doctor, or an executive, with his suit jacket neatly folded across the passenger seat. According to that gold wedding band twinkling in the window frame, he was also a husband.

"How much?" He rubbed his fingers together to make sure I understood he meant money.

I walked over to the car, slow, slinky, the way I imagined the Avenue Foch girls did when getting ready to climb into a car. I bent down to the window, smiling a smile that did not belong to me but to some other girl with solid gold cojones.

"That depends on what you want."

"How much for the ass?" He was practically salivating.

I took a drag on my cigarette and turned my hips toward him.

"This ass?"

He nodded, showing me a wide symmetrical smile that must have cost a fortune.

I leaned into the window.

"This ass will cost you *extra*."

I grabbed his wrist and pressed it firmly on the window frame with one hand, using my free hand to rub my cigarette into the top of his palm while he squealed in pain, trying to pull back his hand, but I was overcome with strength and held on tightly, singeing his pink skin with my cigarette. He called me putain, salope, pétasse, conasse, and many other words I didn't know while I let him burn. Maribel finally grabbed my arm and we ran from the top of Cherche-Midi across the intersection down to rue du Bac before the gendarmes at the Varenne post stopped us, demanding to know why two girls were running in a neighborhood not known for velocity.

"We're just going home," I told them. We weren't but a few meters from our green doors.

"What's that accent?" asked the second gendarme. I could tell he was the one in charge. There is always one in charge.

"It's not any kind of accent. It's the way I talk."

"Why were you running?"

I looked at Maribel, breathless and not much help, and neither of us felt there was any point in telling them the truth.

"We're just going home." I pointed down the road. "We live in the House of Stars."

"Show me your papers."

"We just stepped out for some air," I started, ready to negotiate, but he shook his head and held his finger in the air as if determining the wind.

"Your papers. *Now*."

I'd been warned that I should carry my documentation, though everyone in the neighborhood knew about Séraphine's place and that it was full of girls from all over. But we both had only bank and métro cards on us, which didn't prove our legitimacy enough, so they fined us five hundred francs each, in cash, which they told us we could withdraw from the bank machine around the corner.

"How convenient for you," I told the officer who followed to make sure we didn't make a run for it.

"You should thank me for not arresting you. Foreigners should have their papers on them at all times."

After we handed over the bills, the bossier gendarme said, "If it's true you live in the House of Stars, I want to see you walk into it."

They followed as we made our way to our address, muttering about our culs, and observed as I typed the security pass code into the keypad and pushed open the door to the entrance court. They watched from the sidewalk as we crossed the courtyard and I produced a key and opened our way into the house. As we stepped into the foyer, we turned to face the guards and flipped them off: I, with the American middle finger, and Maribel, Spanish-style, with two fingers and the back of the hand. The gendarmes responded by sticking out their tongues and grabbing their crotches, thrusting in our direction, all of which, I'm sure you know, translates directly.

8

There was this: the sight of him waiting for me by a stone column on the Deauville station platform. The train brakes locked, passengers gathered their bags and filed out, but I waited, wanting to be the last off the train. And there it was, the change, my walking to him, his folding me into his chest, the entwining of the arms, inevitable, and when I pulled away from him, his face was new again. Those dusty eyes turned a radiant green, his cheeks, flushed and dewy. He took my bag in one hand and offered me the other, and we walked together as if this were our routine: my return to a village on the Côte Fleurie. A village I'd never been to, had never known existed until he called that morning to invite me to see him there. And now this place was another room in the home of my life.

"I was afraid you wouldn't come," he said.

When he called that morning to invite me, I'd heard his voice quake with uncertainty, and felt the caution in mine.

"You want me to come today?" I'd wanted him to feel unreasonable, still stung by his sudden departure.

He said I could take the afternoon train. Séraphine was beside me as I spoke. I was the only girl in the house without a personal mobile phone, and the only way he knew to reach me was by call-ing the house line—a number he'd located through his father's secretary—and had called three times before catching me at home. I took the call in her bedroom, and she watched me until I finally said yes, I'd go to him.

We drove from Deauville to Blonville-sur-Mer. Avenues turned to dirt roads ripping through fields of tall grass. In the twi-light it looked to me like the land of Playmobil, brick houses with dark wooden beams, rock walls, sheep, cows like toasted marshmal-lows scattered along rolling green meadows. Dusk folded over the countryside, and in a moment I couldn't pinpoint, I'd found my way out of my world into his.

The house was on the edge of the village, at the end of a forgotten lane lined with empty lots left to birds and other drift-ing animals, just south of a lumpy beach facing England. I heard waves through an open window, across the garden and over the wall lining the property.

"I hope you feel at home here," he said, but the house was quiet and still like my mother's convent, with rooms that felt as if they hadn't been walked through in years.

He showed me to the guest room on the ground floor with white plaster walls adorned with sun-faded flower prints. There was no furniture other than a large iron bed set with embroidered country blankets and a wooden dresser near the door, its drawers empty.

While he went to the garden to fill a canvas sack with fire-wood from a pile in the corner of the yard, I walked through the front rooms of the house, cold at nightfall, sheets covering the rocking chair, the pale blue sofa, and the plaid armchair. A dead room without photographs.

His seemed to me a house that had lost and perhaps hoped to recover.

I searched for evidence of who he was before our meeting. I hoped to find clues of his parentage, the father I'd heard about. The lost mother. I looked for her because I was sure a mother is never really lost. A blue ceramic cross was nailed to a wall in the kitchen on an otherwise bare stucco surface between a cabinet and a window. I imagined his mother placing it there. For protection. For decoration. It was his house now but he kept the cross where she left it.

The kitchen, however, breathed with life, a wooden table at its center holding a bowl of fruit, a tray of vegetables. I pictured him standing over the stove, running water from the faucet. I saw him pull knives from the block, chopping parsley on the wooden board.

Next to the kitchen, a den with a fireplace, toile-papered walls lined with shelves full of books that would be easy tinder if the flames ever grew large enough. On a table along the wall, an old record player. Set on the wooden floorboards, just beyond the frayed gray carpet, a small stereo system. I hadn't seen a television or a telephone anywhere in the house and wondered from where he phoned to invite me. This room did not smell abandoned. The books gathered no dust and the record player held the Rolling Stones' *December's Children*.

I heard the door, his shuffling under the weight of the wood he carried. He called my name.

"I'm here. With your books."

He appeared, his eyes bright. He moved past me and pulled the screen from the fireplace, arranging the wood on the iron nest, pulling a few sheets from the stack of newspaper beside the mantel. He struck a large match on the box at his knees and let the flame burn long and high before lowering the match to a corner of the paper. He coughed. Gently, at first, and then violently, stepping to the window, parting the curtains, lifting the pane, and lowering his head as if starving for fresh air. He seemed delicate to me. I wondered if it was the nature of solitary children. He breathed deeply until his coughing calmed, turning to me on the floor where I sat with my knees pressed to my chest.

"You look so small sitting there."

I told him to come sit beside me, and he pulled some pillows from a stack in the corner, arranging them so we could lean back, eyes on the fire.

"Now you see where I live," he said.

"It's so quiet here." But it was more than silence. A remoteness.

"What's your home like?"

"Crowded," I smiled. How to explain that I grew up in a house more like its own barrio? "It's full of people and animals."

But to tell him how it was now, I had to tell him about my parents, orphans who'd designed their own tribe, and in speaking of them I felt so far from them.

"After my mother died, I would tell people I was an orphan. It was wrong for me to say but that's how it felt even though I still had a father."

He told me he was twelve when she died. His cousin, Sharif, and his mother spent summers at the house with Cato and his mother. The mothers were sisters only a year apart. They left the boys playing at the beach and went to the market to buy food for dinner, their car hit by another, speeding from the direction of the Deauville casinos.

"The police said they were both killed instantly, but it was almost thirty minutes before the medics made it down the ravine."

He shook his head. "I used to tell Sharif I don't think anyone dies in an instant. It must take time for life to leave the body. But Sharif prefers to think they both went out like candles."

After her death, he remained at the house in the care of the Guadeloupian governess named Mireille who helped raise him. She'd recently retired after three decades in France, returning home to Le Gosier to be with her children and their children.

"She wanted me to go with her. She said the Caribbean air would be a good change for me."

"Why didn't you go?"

"I've never wanted to live anywhere but here. I want to die here."

"What about your father? Does he come visit you often?"

"Maybe twice a year. Usually in the summer when the weather is mild."

He looked to the window, then back at me, with a tinge of misgiving. "Do you know about my father?"

"Séraphine told me a little bit."

He sighed as if he'd been expecting this moment.

"My father is a complicated man. His passions are always *against* something. He's the sort of man who must prove his brilliance in every breath."

I thought he sounded a bit like Santi, who made everything a debate.

"How did your parents meet?"

"He was married once before. His first wife died of a brain hemorrhage. They never had children. Many years later my mother was hired as his secretary. He was almost twenty years older than her, and they married after a year together, but he always kept us very separate from his public life. We lived here and he came to see us some weekends and we behaved as a family, but my parents were so different. She was very careful with money, and he spent it like a man who'd never had to work. When he came to visit he took us to expensive restaurants in Deauville, and I remember my mother always looked like a guest at his table."

He looked into the fire and spoke to the flames slowly.

"Sometimes I think I'm the only one who remembers her. It's easier for my father perhaps, because she wasn't the first wife he lost. He tells me I'm too sentimental. He says life goes on, but in many ways it doesn't."

He stood up and left me to climb the wooden stairs, the creaks sharp and loud. He returned, lowered his body onto the cushions, and handed me a large silver frame, lustrous from daily polishing, holding a photograph. Her blonde hair pulled into a loose braid, wearing a straw sunhat, the top frills of a floral dress, her bare freckled shoulders exposed. She had her son's plump lips, the same disorganized smile; she looked happy, but something in her half laugh betrayed that such moments of joy and abandon were rare.

"You must miss her."

"It's strange, when I was a child I loved her so much, as if I already understood that I wouldn't have her for long, and now that she's gone I love her as if she were still alive, just taking too long to come home."

We watched each other.

"It's late," he said. "We should go to sleep."

"What about the fire?" I pointed to it, still smoldering.

"We'll let it burn out."

He led me to the guest room and remained in the doorway while I stood at the center of the room. He said good-bye so softly I might have imagined it, closing the door behind him, and I was alone in the room of dusty flowers. His footsteps echoed up the stairs and then on the floor above me, until it was quiet and I felt him doing just as I was, standing at the foot of the bed, sensing me as I sensed him.

That morning I woke up long before I heard him stir upstairs, waiting in bed as the watery morning light filled the room, the pressed sheets against my bare body, hoping he'd come knocking on the door to wake me, but he didn't. He went from the base of the stairs to the kitchen, filled the kettle with water, moving about the tile floor, teacups clinking. I showered and dressed, wandering with hair dripping down my back to the kitchen. He was at the table, leaning over a newspaper. He wore wire-rim reading glasses, a small new discovery about him that thrilled me.

I asked what was happening in the world but quickly added, "Never mind. Don't tell me. I don't want to know."

During those days, we began a habit of lying together without touching. On the desolate strip of beach just steps from his house. The sun at its noon peak buried into a pastel sky, cold sand under our feet. We wore sweaters, hats, and scarves, stretched on a blanket as waves hit the beaches once stormed by the Allies. He told me he came there every morning and sometimes at sunset through the warmer months. He worked at the marina maintaining boats, washing them, polishing, doing whatever needed to be done. He liked outdoor work. But it wasn't consistent work, because sometimes the boats left for Le Havre or La Rochelle, Cap Ferret or Mallorca, and though it would have been good money, he didn't have the captain's license to transport the boats himself. He'd taken his baccalaureate in history and studied the same in university, but such a degree was only good for indoor jobs. He'd passed the tourism exam, too, but confessed he wasn't very good with people, so he'd never been hired when applying to give D-day tours. He'd had a few friends growing up, but they'd all moved to Paris or other cities by now, for school and for work. And Sharif didn't visit anymore—they only saw each other when Cato went to Paris.

"You have your own corner of the sea here," I said, though it seemed a coast of ghosts with its leftover war tanks and murky foam-capped waves rushing the shore.

"Do you ever get lonely out here?"

"I'm used to solitude," he said. "But yes, now that you're here, I realize I've been very alone."

And then I understood that between us there was a common spore of isolation that grew in my overpopulated home and within his quiet cottage. We were young but we'd both grown well into our loneliness. We were the kind of lonely that wasn't ashamed to be so. A lonely without self-penitence.

We didn't speak of tomorrow when I'd leave on an afternoon train. We didn't make plans. We ate dinner together in the kitchen and when we were finished I peeled an orange from the bowl and gave him half.

Afterward, we lay on the pillows before the cracking fire that warmed the room so much that we pulled off our sweaters and socks, down to our loose jeans and T-shirts. The conversation turned to whispers. His fingertips—nails short, but unbitten—moved to my hand, playing with my fingers, kneading my knuckles like rosary beads, then glided over the terrain of my face. He would come to see me in Paris soon, he said. He kissed me, and then again for a long time. I remember the sight of us as if I were floating above, two sleeping figures by the fire, faces sharing a cushion, toes touching, torsos bowed into each other.

A lifetime without hearing the name de Manou and now I saw and heard it everywhere. When I opened my balcony doors for the last cigarette of the evening, I'd hear Saira's television above echoing with the nightly news. The report of the day's strikes, the week's national complaints, the name Antoine de Manou followed by a sound byte of a raspy, gurgled voice heaving that France no longer belonged to the French. "We," meaning the French, needed to reclaim it, close its doors to foreigners responsible for crime, unemployment, drugs, and riots. De Manou couldn't get through a sentence without pausing to clear his throat, swallowing saliva so much that he was regularly satirized in the form of a drooling dog-faced puppet on *Les Guignols*.

His far-right party had come in third for popularity in last spring's elections; the opposition commentators argued that de Manou represented Old France and New France should be progressive, seek solutions beyond the fueling of old resentments. Then the news would cut back to the studio reporter who'd wrap up with the question: Would Antoine de Manou run for president again? He'd run twice already and not won. Was he too old? With France in crisis, on the cusp of transitioning from the franc to the euro, would de Manou's party gain strength or become obsolete like in the MC Solaar song?

The newspaper stand at the fused arteries of rue du Bac, boulevard Saint Germain, and boulevard Raspail displayed front pages featuring de Manou's tirades on banning headscarves and traditional robes in the classroom, cultural clues that distracted from his vision of the *Ideal Authentic France*. He had ideas like turning certain banlieues into closed colonies, increasing deportations, and banning nationalization for children of immigrants. The year before, he'd even remarked that Les Bleues, the French national soccer team, a majority of them minorities, didn't reflect the *true* France. Under the headlines, a photograph of a well-dressed gentleman or a madman, pig-nosed and large-eyed with spotted cheeks and tubular lips that flapped outward showing his old gums and false teeth. A man under the weight of decades of accusations of committing torture in Algeria for which he'd never been tried because, as Séraphine said, the French have a long memory for some things and a short memory for others.

He was all wrinkles and creases, with bags under his eyes and a shiny head, bald but for a few stubborn threads and fuzzy patches above his ears, only useful for holding his thick black glasses in place.

I searched those newspaper and magazine portraits for traces of his son but couldn't find any.

On days that I stopped in a café with Loic or some of the other girls, I'd catch his name in conversation at a nearby table or find a paper that had been left behind on the banquette; a cover photo of the contorted face of Le Vieux de Manou with one of his preferred slogans—*Aliens Out!* or *True France! Pure France!*—printed above his head. It didn't matter the neighborhood or the venue, de Manou's unyielding fight against a tainted nation was on the public's lips, and I wished I could return to my former ignorance, when the only de Manou I knew was the one who asked me if I was lost.

*   *   *

I met him at Gare Saint-Lazare just after sunset. It was dark and cold, even through my warmest jacket, a knit hat, and scarf, with only a patch of face open to the air. I was disappointed by the size of his bag, big enough for only two or three days of travel. We kissed in the taxi all the way to the Seventh, had dinner at Le Perron, and walked to the House of Stars, which was quiet, all the others out for a Friday night, only the sound of Saira's television buzzing on the floor above us.

I let him into my bedroom ahead of me while I closed the door and leaned against the frame. He dropped his bag by my desk and looked at the photographs taped to the wall, stepping in to get a closer look at my family, standing next to Eden's burial rosebush behind my mother's old convent.

"I like your room." Strange to hear him say it as I felt he'd been there before.

"There's not much space," I said. My bed looked very small pushed into the corner, and I suddenly felt improper.

I'd wondered how this would go. Would we fall onto the bed in mad passion or would there be hesitation? In his house there was the buffer of an extra bedroom, but here it was my small room and the even smaller bed.

Then, the quiet embarrassment of changing out of my clothes and into a T-shirt and shorts. He sensed my clumsy modesty and turned away without my asking. I wanted to be like Tarentina with a wardrobe of glamorous nightclothes, walking around in her lingerie, baring her body without inhibition. But I hid myself, sliding into the bed and pulling the blanket over me while he removed his shirt and I took in his lithe body, almost hairless thin skin, muscles long and liquid, his chest slightly concave. He kept on his jeans, reaching over to turn off the nightstand light, lifting the blanket only enough to slip in beside me.

We lay like planks. My body adjusted to his warm arms against mine in the purest blindness of night. The room came into soft focus. Dots of stars over the rooftops beyond the windows, blue moonlight hitting the corners of the room. I turned my head enough to see his profile, the bridge of his nose, the rise and dips of his mouth and chin sloping down to the plateau of his chest. I held my breath, trying to be inconspicuous in my desire, but by the next breath he was above me, and then the removal of my shirt, the jeans, the underclothes.

We stayed in bed for days, only leaving to refill a water bottle at the bedside, steal leftover food from the kitchen, or use the bathroom. The maids knocked. The other girls spoke to me through the door. I told them to go away. Violeta shouted through the hinges that she needed to clean, but I liked the smell of us filling the room, opening the balcony doors each morning for a flush of air. Loic banged on the door demanding to know if I was alive. I finally opened it a crack and saw Tarentina and Maribel watching from behind him.

"Yes, I'm alive." I felt Cato's hand on mine, pulling me back to him. *Never more alive.*

"Séraphine is concerned that she hasn't seen you in days. She wants you to come down to see her when you have a chance."

"Yes, when I have a chance." But I'd already relocated. I lived in that room with him now. The bed was our house. The rug, our garden.

We told each other stories, filling the emptiness of the years spent waiting. I told him of my family, my race through school, running on guilt for the debt of my parents' hardships, my life a project in honoring their sacrifices, how I never felt that my life belonged only to me but to them and I sometimes resented it, which made me ashamed. I told him about my brothers, one with a warrior gene, born for an army my mother would never let him join, and the other, a wounded soul, deemed so helpless that one of our dogs, a German shepherd named Ramses, had been specially trained to watch over him so he wouldn't hurt himself.

He told me that as a boy he'd had a German shepherd, too. His mother had named her Anastasia and she'd slept at his side, licking his fingers to wake him for school. But his father hated animals, and when he visited, Anastasia was forced to stay outside. Cato sneaked her in from the yard to sleep in his room. When his father came in the morning and saw the dog on the bed, he took it by the collar, dragged it down the stairs, put it in his car, and drove away. When Cato asked what happened to Anastasia, he was always told different things—that his father gave the dog away to another family, that he left her by the road, that he took the dog to a field and shot her. The last possibility, he said, the most likely.

I tried to conceal my shock as he pressed further into my embrace.

I told him I'd never had friends in school. They thought me too strange. The only friend I did have was Ajax, who seemed to quietly hate me so much that once, because I wouldn't give him money for drugs, he tried to stab me with a pocketknife my father gave him when he took us all fishing in the Poconos. And then there was Daniel. But ours was juvenile affection, born out of proximity more than desire.

Cato considered Sharif lucky; his father's Moroccan family in Paris took him in even though his father went back to Morocco fifteen years ago and hadn't been allowed to reenter France. Sharif had plenty of aunts, uncles, and other cousins in France, so he didn't need Cato as much as Cato needed him. Sharif had also discovered a passion for graffiti soon after their mothers died, a reason to stay on the streets rather than go home and remember that his mother was no longer there waiting for him.

"But I'm the opposite. After my mother died it was hard for me to leave my house. It still is."

"Was it hard for you to leave to come here?"

"Yes. But I'm happy I came. I've been following you around in my mind since the night I met you."

We were still new to each other, transcribing the weight of each other's flesh to our bones. The eyes and the wounds and the longing living beneath them would always be new until we were old and by then being old would be new. I ran my palm from his chest over the ridges of his ribs to his navel. My finger dipped into a crescent scar in its orbit. I loved scars; I was covered in them from countless falls as a distracted child, chasing Santi through the woods as we played Indios and Españoles.

"What is this scar from?"

"I was sick as a child," he said, his eyes suddenly heavy with what looked like fatigue or regret. "My throat closed and I became very skinny, so they inserted a tube there."

"A tube?"

"To feed me."

He put his finger over mine, slipping it over the scar.

"What did you have?"

"Bad lungs."

"Like asthma?"

"In a way."

I kissed his mouth. I told him we were all sick as children, ill with childhood, invalids in a world of indelicate adults with the wrong prognoses and cures.

We made love again. Afterward he said, as if it were a long time ago, "I remember when I saw you by the torch that night. You were wearing that blouse with the dragon on the back."

"It was borrowed."

"I knew it. By the way you wore it I knew it wasn't yours. I wondered, Why is she wearing a shirt that doesn't belong to her? That's why I talked to you. I never speak to strange people. Especially to a girl standing alone on a street corner in the middle of the night. In this city, that's only looking for trouble. But I saw the dragon before I saw your face, and when I walked beside you on the bridge and saw your eyes, so suspicious of me, I knew I liked you."

"I'm still suspicious of you."

"I still like you. Very much."

There was something in his sweet first impressions. Those willful projections. I wondered if we were whom the other hoped. He hadn't yet said when he would leave. So I pretended he was here forever. There was no morning, only this perpetual hour, this room warm with our breath and sweat, these sheets pushed off the bed, this silence of two bare bodies.

9

I began having lofty visions that made me a little afraid of myself. Visions of things I never knew I wanted. To be married. To make a life. To have a home together; a twofold narcissism leaving me self-conscious of how I held his hand when we walked along the chilly streets, not wanting to be one of those girls clinging to her lover like a monkey on a palm or, like Maribel, who crumpled like papier-mâché into Florian's side, but a couple who held each other with equal possession.

We eventually began a more practical routine, emerging from our seclusion to join the others for meals in the house kitchen when Giada would cook a pot of pasta for all the residents, or at Far Niente. I observed as Cato became friendlier with Rachid and Stef, who were also unlike the majority of swaggering boys who passed through the house, wallets full of cash and credit cards, lives fueled by a pipeline of connections. I was pleased the others, even Tarentina, had accepted him into their ranks, and though he wasn't one for crowds, I noticed his gentle way with people, slowly disarming, truthful, ingenuous. They teased him for never wanting to join the group out at the nightclubs or for not staying beyond one beer at Claude's before complaining about the smoke, calling him a country boy. But Cato didn't seem to mind, and I enjoyed that rather than experiencing Paris nightlife, he preferred to be home with me.

Even Romain warmed to Cato, and on slow nights at Far Niente when he had nothing to do but pull up a chair and join us at our preferred long corner table, I watched them talk about growing up by the sea, and the beast of city life.

I had term paper orders to fulfill for the girls and their friends, and during those hours, Cato would read on my bed while I worked at the desk or go out with Sharif and, occasionally, to visit his father. Romain started turning up again for his reading sessions, pronouncing with more fluidity and confidence, and though he'd been a bit removed those first days, we both settled back into our reading routine.

When we arrived at the part when Martin and Ruth fall in love, Romain dropped the book into his lap.

"Help me to understand something, Lita. Something I've been wondering about for a while now."

"What is it?"

"What exactly are you doing with Antoine de Manou's kid?"

I wasn't surprised the news had reached him but was taken aback by the contempt in his voice.

"What is that supposed to mean?"

"I'm just . . ." he screwed his lips into a sneery pout. ". . . surprised."

"Surprised at what? You seem to be getting along with him just fine."

"I just thought . . ."

"You just thought what?"

"I thought you would've had more integrity than to fall for the son of a savage."

"He's nothing like his father."

"*Every* man is like his father."

"Well, your father is a butcher. So what does that make you?"

"It's not the same. People have to eat."

"And your father is happy to deal in cadavers."

He let out a low whistle. "Incredible. Only two months in France and you've already been converted to de Manou's party. Your parents will be so proud."

"He's not for you to judge. You barely know him."

"As do you."

"I think I know him better than you do."

"I'm sorry to tell you this, but it takes more than a few weeks in bed together to know a man."

If he hadn't been one of my first friends in Paris I would have kicked him out, but I only stood up to search my desk drawer for an old pack of cigarettes, untouched since Cato's arrival because he didn't smoke or like the smell of it.

"Believe me, Romain, there are many other ways I'd rather spend my afternoons than reading a novel I've already read in slow motion with you. And all you want is to insult me?"

"It's not insults. It's honesty. Why are Americans so sensitive?"

I opened the balcony doors and leaned on the railing, putting as much space as I could between Romain and me, though he took it as a cue to follow me and now stood beside me, pulling a cigarette from his own pack and lighting it close to my face.

"You girls are all the same." His exhale of smoke hit my cheek. "You say you came to Paris to become educated and cultured. You say you want to be women of the world but all you really want is a boyfriend."

"Don't tell me you've never been in love."

"Too many times, actually. But I don't plan on letting it happen again. Love is a distraction. It steals time, talent, focus, and turns great minds to mush. It's a perfect waste."

"You sound like you've had your heart broken."

"Me? Never. I'm the one who does the breaking. But it does hurt to be the one leaving sometimes. I won't deny that."

"Well, then, you have it all figured out."

He rubbed his stub into the ashtray on the railing between us and offered me an expression I could see he'd learned from acting, a face that asked to be forgiven for being naughty.

"So," he said, when we'd settled back onto the floor. "Where is the Little Prince this afternoon anyway?"

"Don't call him that. He's having lunch with his father."

"And does Papa know his son has taken up residence with you?"

I tapped the book cover in his hands. "Just read, will you?"

"He's not ashamed of you, is he?" He was grinning, so I tried to take it as a joke, kicking him across the carpet until he caught my foot with his hand and finally started reading again.

But the question lingered.

A few nights later, over jasmine tea and brochettes at Tokyo-rama, when Cato mentioned that he'd stopped by his father's place that afternoon, I took the opportunity to ask, casually, as if it hadn't been on my mind for days, "Does he know you're staying with me?"

"He assumes I'm staying with Sharif. But he doesn't like him, so he never asks."

"Are you hiding me?" I hated myself for asking.

"No." He took a long breath, watching me with eyes that asked for patience.

"One day you will meet him, Lita. And you will understand everything."

Cato went back to Blonville-sur-Mer for a few days in early November to get some warmer clothes. Even so, we'd mostly stopped venturing into the white-breath night because it made his back ache and worsened his subtle, never-departing cough. Sometimes those coughs turned into heaving gasps that left him hunched over, supporting himself on the hood of a parked car. I thought he should see a doctor but didn't have one to recommend, only knew of the doctors who came to see Séraphine or the ones the other girls visited for their birth control pills. It didn't occur to me that his father must have had access to the best doctors in the country.

On an unseasonably mild day in December I had the idea to go to the Palais Royal. Earlier in the afternoon, we'd gone to see the new Tony Gatlif movie about a French guy who ends up living among a Roma community and ultimately falls for the pretty gypsy girl, which I thought was a predictable story line, and Cato didn't disagree with me, but that's because I was being difficult and he was being careful. For weeks, the house had rustled with holiday chatter, the girls' plans for their glamorous getaways while I'd be the only one going home for the break. Cato said he usually spent Christmas with his father and the new year with Sharif's family in Goutte d'Or, so that morning, as we dressed, I extended what I thought was a casual invitation.

"You know, you could come to the States and spend the holidays with me and I could introduce—"

"I can't go."

"Why not?"

"It's not easy for me to travel like it is for you," he said and, reading my thoughts, added, "and it's got nothing to do with money."

"But—"

"I can't, Lita. I just can't."

There was a coolness between us for the rest of the day, on the walk to the theater and the bus ride to the Palais Royal. Just the night before, in the midst of the House of Stars' winter party, it occurred to me that I'd never been happier in all my life than I was with Cato, even with his reticence about the holidays. Fewer people were invited to this party because, with the bone chill, we were confined indoors, but the house was ripe with laughter, lovers tucked into corners, girls and boys meeting each other for the first time, and Cato beside me. The night concluded like so many others, with us cloistered in Tarentina's room, passing around the shisha pipe. Rachid dismantled a cigarette, removing the filter and some tobacco, packing the gaps with a smidge of hashish tar, chased by another spliff folded with the Turkish weed Giada brought back from her last weekend in Berlin. The joints went around the group three or four times. I never took a turn, hearing my father's doctrine that to dabble is to dip one's hands in the blood of many nations. But by the fifth round that night, I relented and went in for a hit. Then, for the first time since I'd known him, Cato reached for one, too. But when Sharif looked up from his conversation with Rachid, he lurched across the circle of crossed legs to snatch it from Cato's lips. Everyone laughed, but I saw from Sharif's twisted brows that it wasn't meant to be comical. He muttered something too quick for me to understand, followed by something in Arabic that only Rachid and maybe Dominique would have caught if they'd been paying attention, which they were not.

The next day in the Palais Royal, as we made our way through the corridor of the Galerie de Valois, Cato collapsed beside me.

I caught him before he hit the ground, holding him and screaming for help in all my languages while Cato choked on his own breath, his face reddening and whitening. He managed to pull his wallet from his jeans pocket, opening the front flap to show me a medical card, which I gave to the medics when they arrived, and just before they covered his face with an oxygen bubble, pulling him off me onto an orange plastic stretcher, he gasped my name.

I waited for more, but he looked at me as if I were a mere stranger who'd picked him up, pushing out the words, "Call my father."

Later, when I got ahold of him, Sharif would tell me it happened the same way during his last attack four years ago. Cato knew better, he said. It was the smoke from the night before, which we'd all held into our chests and released with ease and laughter, full of latent fungi that ignited spores on Cato's cystic lungs. He was sick long before I met him. Sharif said we could blame the winds of Chernobyl. Sharif and Cato were eleven at the time of the toxic disaster, vacationing with their mothers in Bretagne when the radioactive cloud and subsequent rains passed over them. Until a few years earlier, Cato's father headed the committee denying the rumored health effects of the blast on children in France.

Cato was one of many, Sharif said. It had started with a cancer. A nodule on his thyroid that was removed. Hadn't I noticed the faded white seam of stitches at the base of his neck?

"I've only got an irregular thyroid I control with daily medication," Sharif said. "Cato got it much, much worse."

After the cancer, pulmonary sarcoidosis. Some live with it, unaffected, but it made Cato inhumanly susceptible to dust and bacteria. Where the average person's lungs heal with a diminutive scar, his grew fibrous tissue. Sharif said Cato had arthritis and was in pain all the time. Hadn't I noticed the steroids he took every day, the orange inhaler he carried in his pocket? Sharif insisted Paris was too much for Cato—he needed the purest oxygen nature could offer.

"Why else," he said, "do you think he would choose to live all alone in that house on the edge of the world?"

I closed my eyes as if that would change anything and saw only Cato. His temperate negotiations to avoid going in the métro—claustrophobia, he said—or join the others when they invited us to smoke-filled nightclubs and parties. The mornings when he woke up almost blue, coughing, blaming it on the dust in the old House of Stars, I thought only of the lazy maids, not of how I'd once teased, "You look like a corpse when you sleep," and he hadn't laughed.

Loic drove me to the American Hospital in Neuilly every day to see if I could get past the nurses who'd been instructed to turn away visitors. On the eighth day he was released to his father's care. Sharif convinced Monsieur de Manou to let me visit, explaining that I was respectable, one of the House of Stars girls, and on the eleventh day, after the office of Monsieur de Manou called Séraphine to verify this fact, I was given an appointment.

Antoine de Manou's apartment occupied the entire third floor of an elegant building on rue Vaneau. A young butler in a white jacket showed me to the sitting room. The walls were lined with plaques and dignitary portraits of the suited elder de Manou standing with other decorated men in posed handshakes, and older photos of him in military clothing, wearing medals, gazing meditatively over some foreign landscape. I heard muffled voices in another room followed by footsteps in the corridor, and then a thin woman in a tailored dress suit with a narrow avian face arrived in the doorway, waving me toward her. She didn't introduce herself and only looked straight ahead as she led me down the hall, warning, "You'll have thirty minutes with Felix. You must not touch him or allow your voice to rise above the level of a whisper. You may be alarmed when you see him. He's sedated for his comfort."

We turned into another hall where a nurse sat on a chair outside a door, knitting a shapeless gray mass. She nodded at both of us, and the thin woman pushed open the door and left me to walk in on my own.

He was lying in a frameless bed, flat, covered by a white blanket, surrounded by buzzing monitors, cables running along his arms and under his sheet, electric buds taped to his bruised chest. His nose and mouth were covered by a breathing mask, his eyes closed in what resembled a peaceful sleep despite the needles lodged in his veins.

Two more nurses watched over him and the machines from his bedside. One of them stood up so I could sit. She was an older lady, from Slovakia, she told me, when I later asked.

"Felix," she said in a naturally coarse voice that tried hard to be soft, "your friend is here to see you."

She touched my arm. "He can hear you."

I didn't speak. I didn't touch him. I didn't reach under the sheet so he could feel my hand. I only observed the outline of his body under the cotton shroud, those motionless arms and legs that I'd believed were created to be wrapped around me. How badly I wanted to share with him that, in the days since he collapsed, I'd worn his clothes, slept in the dirty shirts he'd left piled on the chair in the corner of our room. I wore his gray sweater with the frayed hem and hole under the arm that day. I wondered if he knew it, if he could smell himself on me.

In those days of anxious waiting, Tarentina had taken me aside and told me, "This is life telling you it's time to walk away."

I searched Cato's eyelids for the movement of dreams but they were still.

The old man stopped me as I stepped out of his foyer into the building hall to head home. He was shorter and more blockish than I expected and I could see clear over his square bald head, through the few hard white hairs combed over his spotted scalp. He wore a brown suit, periwinkle shirt, and orange tie.

"Lucrecia," he began.

"Leticia," I said, but he didn't acknowledge my clarification, and instead stared back as if I'd insulted him.

"Do you know who I am?"

"You're Cato's father."

"Yes, and it is because Felix is my son that I must share with you that your interest in his well-being is touching but unnecessary. You may be assured that as my son he receives superior medical care. Your presence, while you might think it comforting, is a nuisance, a distraction, and thus we might consider it . . . debilitating. Am I making myself clear?"

He swayed when he spoke, trembling from the neck, without taking a breath, so that his words sounded thin, never rising or falling in tone, as if reading from a prompter, not looking at me but through me.

"I'm not sure I understand, sir."

"Well then, let me try it this way. Until Felix's cousin brought your name to my attention, I had never heard of you. You can determine for yourself what this says about your friendship with my son."

I was silent as he took a step into the hall toward me, his nostrils expanding.

"Now that you have seen he is safe and well cared for, I am sure you will understand when I tell you that there is no need for you to return."

With that, he stepped back into his home and shut the door.

10

My mother and I sat together on the window seat in my childhood bedroom. I looked through the glass to the backyard, grass
turned gray, dying of winter, and the Christmas lights brightening
trees and bushes under the pale northeastern sunset. It seemed
my parents had aged more rapidly in the four months I was away,
but now that she had me alone, my mother said it was I who'd
aged, looking both thin and bloated, ashy with inverted halos
darkening my eyes.

I'd wanted to stay with him in Paris. On the plane ride
home, I told myself I'd get used to this feeling of my soul divided.
My body would show up for Navidad with la familia, and my
unseen self would remain with him, on a horizon I saw scrawled
with our names the way he'd written them into the shoulder of
the bronze statue on the Pont Alexandre, the way I'd scribbled
them into the inner covers of my diary, drawn them onto my dry
skin with my jagged fingernails, traced them into the cool flesh
of his back as he hovered over me in the bruise-blue darkness of
my Paris bedroom.

I was picked up at the airport by all my family, but was numb
as my father's car negotiated one highway packed with holiday

traffic onto another, the strip malls lined with flashing red and green lights, glittering garlands, fat Santas, and cartoonish reindeer in storefront windows.

I had to tell my mother about him in a way that wouldn't scare her. She was already uncertain of her motherhood, often doubting herself, relying more on prayers than her own wisdom to guide me. She'd once confessed to me that she didn't know how to be a parent. She felt like an overgrown orphan who'd never learned the methods of motherhood. A lioness acting on instinct over reason.

I described a boy and a girl who met among friends by the river on a warm late summer night.

"His father is a distinguished man," I said, the polite way, Séraphine told me, of referring to men of a certain status, but my mother didn't understand and waited for more.

"He's an *important* man."

I told her Cato's mother had died and about his childhood in the countryside, and that his father lived near the House of Stars.

We watched each other.

My mother was already a mother at my age. Now she was tired yet striking in her rugged wild way. Her eyes had fallen a bit since I last saw her. Her firm lips had thinned. I moved to stand up and leave her alone on the window seat, but she touched my hand lightly and I was still. I wanted to tell her it finally happened: The elusive love-knowledge she'd described to me when I was a child was now mine. But her eyes said beware—the same look she gave me long ago when I'd fallen in love with Daniel and she told me quietly, as we chopped vegetables together for the dinner soup, "Nobody tells you that when you give yourself completely to someone, you never get all of yourself back."

I had thrown her advice back in her face.

"That's because you've only loved one man in your life."

A man who'd loved her out of her girlhood and away from her country.

But my mother wasn't cruel or punishing the way other mothers can be, and responded only by picking up her cutting board to slide the tomatoes into the pot on the stove before coming back to her place at the counter beside me.

"I'm only saying that in life there are illusions and sometimes you don't discover what they are until many years later."

We arrived an hour early to claim our seats for the midnight Mass. My mother spent the waiting time on her knees, eyes shut, her knuckles laced with her favorite rosary, which my father made for her out of nails as a wedding gift. He leaned back into the pew, glancing around at the other parishioners, up at the vaulted ceiling. Santi and his girlfriend of one year, Priscilla, daughter of Salvador, the famous painter of skeletal condors from Bucaramanga, held hands, stealing an occasional kiss on the lips with an eye on my mother to make sure she was still praying.

Priscilla wanted to marry my brother, but Santi wasn't yet sure. She was twenty-three and told him she was a virgin upon meeting him, thinking it would make him more interested. She spoke openly of her maternal cravings, her lack of ambition for anything but keeping a house. She cooked desserts for our family and made her breasts and thighs the highlight of every outfit. Next to her I was plain and boyish. She didn't understand why I worked so hard in school. She said men don't like so much education and that literature, art, and history were for depressives.

"Men are fragile, Lita. A woman's role is to baby them, not be smarter than them."

When I told her I was going away to France, she said a woman shouldn't travel alone except to visit her relatives.

"You are not from this century," I told her, but she only laughed and said that being modern means knowing the old ways work best.

"I'm going to marry your brother," she added, fully confident in her words. "I'm going to marry him because I deserve it."

I sat between her and Beto, who was dressed in a suit he'd inherited from Santi, tailored down to his thin frame, the jacket still sliding off his shoulders, making him look even more of a child. He'd instantly forgiven me for leaving him with a welcome-back hug at the airport. He was already half into a nap, but our mother wouldn't scold him because it was a side effect of his new medication and we were supposed to be happy he could sit through his classes now without running out of the room to call her, begging her to pick him up and take him home.

When I looked at him in his current state, with his glazed stare, I was nostalgic for the angry daggers he threw my way when I left for Paris. I worried for who we had become. And I wondered if I was medicating myself with my own half-life in Paris, the narcotic of romance, afforded by all the years our parents had starved to give me the privilege.

After Mass, Beto held my arm as we walked down the path from the church to the parking lot, the chill burning our eyes. Our parents walked ahead of us, in matching steps, holding hands to keep each other from slipping on the dark ice.

"It wasn't only me having a hard time with you away," Beto told me. "They were the ones crying. Especially Mami. Every day."

Our father was expressive and emotional, but our mother never shed tears, as though she'd never learned how. I was sure Beto was exaggerating.

"I don't believe you. She never cries."

"Santi says she never had to before because we were always there."

When I later asked Santi about it, he told me, "I keep having to explain to them that your self-discovery crap is an American thing. They're just enduring it until you come back to us to do what you're meant to do."

"And what's that?"

"What you've always done. Help Mami with her charity work and come work at Compa' with Pa and me."

"Did they tell you that?"

"They didn't have to."

"But what if that's not what I want?"

"Oye, where's your loyalty? You're not an amoeba. You didn't come into this world alone. Our viejos gave us so much, the least we can do is put everything we gained back into our own family. Jesus, Lita. You're such a gringa sometimes."

"I just want to know, when exactly does my life belong to me?"

"Are you kidding? *Never*."

On Christmas Day, the del Cielo house filled with dozens of friends eating, and singing along with guitars and accordions, the songs of our parents' childhood. Our neighbor Abel got weepy every Christmas, after the first glass of wine, counting the family members he'd lost to war and disease, through the years of living an ocean apart, the wife he never found, the children he never had, saying immigration was a lonely business when you had nobody to share it with. By sunset he was moaning as he often did into my father's shoulder that when he was old and frail there would be no one to take care of him. He said he envied my father and may God have mercy on him for his terrible, terrible jealousy and greed, because he was a poor man who became a rich man only to learn that true fortune is family.

By the end of the night, my parents, in the face of opulent gift-giving and extravagant quantities of food, began reminiscing about their former poverty, when they could live for a week on five dollars, made soups of whatever they could find so they could spend it on food for baby Santi, now six foot three, muscular, and clear eyed. I tried to picture Cato among us, tried to imagine how the worlds I'd tried to separate to this point would, if I let them, converge.

My father woke each morning at five without an alarm and made rounds, checking on his sleeping children who were no longer children, made the first pot of coffee, fed the animals, then returned to his room to do calisthenics on the floor, concluding with fifty push-ups on his ever-shrinking biceps. When I was small, I'd wake as soon as I heard his footsteps and go sit on the floor and watch him, the straightness of his tan bare back sloping into his pajama pants, his thin arms pulsing under his body weight. It hurt me to watch him as he struggled through the last few presses, his face flushed, his neck veins bulging. It showed the limits of his strength and filled me with terror that someday something more powerful than my father might break him.

That morning when I heard his soft steps on the wood floors, I got up to meet him in the hall and followed him around for his ritual. He whispered good morning to the dogs, who met his legs with affectionate nose rubs, the waiting cats, their tails popped like poles as he freshened their water bowls and replenished their food.

He saw me standing in the doorway. "You're still on Paris time, corazón?"

"You know I'm an early riser, Pa."

I wanted to tell him about Cato but knew my father would say, "People don't fall in love like it's a hole in the ground. Love is not an accident. Love doesn't arrive or drop from the sky like rain. Love is a carefully prepared meal between two people who will sit and eat together."

And a choice that should be made very carefully because, according to him, we are each the sum of the people we love. He chose my mother because they had lived a similar story, a blanket of hunger and shame covering each of their childhoods. Neither of them had anything, and they thought that, together, they might make *something*.

"Only rich people and fools have time to sit around thinking about love. And we are not rich people no matter how much money we have to keep us from going hungry. We will always be poor people, and the day I or any of my children believe we are rich is the day we go blind and the day we go blind is the day I begin to die."

"How do you know when you've found love?" I'd asked my father many times throughout my childhood, trying to understand the mysterious fate that led my parents to each other.

"There has to be a moment, Papi, when you're sure of it, isn't there?"

"You don't 'find' love, mi amor. You *choose* it. And then to keep love, you must choose it again, day after day."

When I called, Sharif told me Cato was awake most of the day now. He and the nurses mentioned I'd been there to see him but Cato didn't respond.

"He didn't ask for me?"

"No." Sharif turned quiet and behind him I heard the noise of his household, in Goutte d'Or. "You have to understand, Lita. The last time this happened, the silence didn't leave him for months."

By the time I returned to France, Cato was already home by the sea. I didn't know how to contact him there, so I went on my own, boarding the train at Gare Saint-Lazare, hailing a taxi at the station in Calvados, guiding the driver to his house by memory since I didn't have the address.

He opened the door to me and there were no words. I rushed into him, his diminishing frame against my rib cage.

"Please," he spoke into my hair, "let's not talk about it," and though I wasn't sure if he meant his illness or what had become of us in the silence of our time apart, I nodded.

It was my first time in his bedroom. I remember thinking it had the feeling of a bunker. It faced the back of the house and had a large three-pane window with a view to the garden, which was often blocked by the thick toile curtains he'd open for only an hour a day to clear out the stale air. He didn't care for daylight, and his room was further darkened by stacks of books and several wooden trunks pushed against the eggshell walls. A large map of the flattened earth was pinned to one, rumpled and sagging. The four-poster bed was neatly made with crisp white sheets and a navy coverlet. An old rotary telephone on the floor beside the bed attached to an answering machine. His shoes lined the wall by the door, an order to the disorder, even if my first sight of the room filled me with an overwhelming sorrow, as if he'd moved the totality of his life into these walls.

He welcomed me, made room for me, by moving things aside and unfolding a rack for me to place my bag on, clearing space in his closet for me to hang the few clothes I'd brought with me. I went to the window and pushed the curtains apart. My first effort was to fill the room with the noise of conversation, ask for anecdotes about the origin of everything, and he obliged at first but became winded from speaking and eased himself onto the bed. I lay beside him. I kissed him, but he fell into a fit of coughs and I rushed down to the kitchen for a glass of water. I wanted it to be as it was before, to sleep naked with him, feel his skin, his hot breath, but it was cold both outside and in his room. We slept in sweaters and pants, our feet wrapped in thick wool socks his mother knitted long ago. I reached for him throughout the night. I didn't sleep, but he did, heavily, and I resisted shaking him awake until morning bled into afternoon.

I made a large breakfast of eggs, sausages, toast, and coffee. When a woman who lived down the road brought vegetables and food for him that morning, I met her at the door. She looked me over and asked how long I'd been working for Monsieur.

"I'm not his employee," I answered. "I'm his guest."

I tried to make light of it later, joking to Cato that maybe the woman with the vegetables thought I was his new governess.

"It's an understandable error. There has never been another girl who stayed here with me. You're the first."

He sat at the table and faced my meal with resignation. He had little appetite and said his throat still ached from the tubes, his chest still burned with pressure. But he took a few bites of the eggs before pushing the plate away, promising he'd eat more later.

While he rested in the afternoon, I cleaned the house, dusting the furniture and shelves, washing the windows and floors, exorcising as I fluffed the pillows and cushions, straightened the books and records. I found a bicycle in the garage covered in cobwebs, cleaned it, found an air pump in a junk pile and filled the tires. I rode down the pebbled road to the row of shops by the marina, a few people gathered around the wooden stand where the fishermen sold their daily catch. I waited my turn, then asked the fisherman for two fillets, but he pretended he couldn't hear me and tended to a woman who arrived after me. I tried again, and again I was ignored. I pulled back and watched as each person in the small crowd was acknowledged and served, walking away with their paper-wrapped bundle of fish.

I was used to living with a continuous case of mistaken identity. Not only in Paris when someone took me for a hooker or followed me around a store, but almost every time I got in a taxi, the driver, whether French, African, Spanish, Italian, or Arab, assumed I was a Maghreb girl. When I said I wasn't, I'd often get hit with insults for denying my culture and thinking I was superior just because I was in France now. It wasn't so different from life back home, growing up in an affluent yet sheltered ivory village, with no idea I wasn't what the standardized forms called White until informed by my third-grade teacher. No one is born with the feeling of not belonging. It's thrust upon us. But it was a condition I was already used to, and most of the time I barely noticed it.

But this time, I thought of Cato's father. I'd decided I'd never tell Cato how he'd dismissed me from his home when I came to see him ill, but now, I felt the old man everywhere, in the faces of the market people, the fishmonger, the woman delivering the basket of vegetables, and their eyes deeming me unworthy, invisible. Yet it wasn't hurt that I felt, but confusion, unsure if I was who I thought I was. But, I told myself, all that mattered was who Cato and I were in relation to each other.

That night, I ran the hot water and let the bathroom fill with steam until the walls were covered in vapor. When the tub was full and warm, I invited him in and we both settled into the water, our legs tangled, knees peaking above the surface. I washed his hair. Ran the razor along his neck to his face until he was smooth all over, his eyes closed, cheeks soft and shiny. When I put down the blade, he smiled, moving forward to kiss me, but his coughing stopped him. I held him into my chest. We stayed this way until the water turned cold. I pulled myself out and let him look at me. The room glowed amber and gold as the bathwater dripped from my skin to the tile floor. Even in my room in Paris I'd always stayed in the shadows or with a sheet pulled over me. Here, I stood before him.

I brought him a towel and held it as he climbed out of the tub, shivering into my arms. In the bed, he approached my body with new vigor, the sheets and blankets kicked to the floor. The moon shone through the curtains making an indigo valley of the bedroom, starlight carving out corners among the books and trunks, my flattened duffel bag forgotten on the floor.

Weeks passed this way.

I pretended I was a wife. I pretended he was my husband. I pretended one day there would be a child sleeping quietly on the bed between us.

We began the New Year together, a Saint-Sylvestre feast for two of oysters and champagne, though we missed the strike of midnight by an hour, the house quiet except for our voices. I've never believed in resolutions, only in desires and decisions, and told him so, but did as I would have done at home with my family. The tradition was to coat the grapes in sugar and pluck and eat a succession of twelve at the midnight we'd claimed for ourselves. We didn't share our wishes but swallowed them silently with our eyes on each other. We stayed awake until sunrise and put on our warmest clothes for a walk along the water's edge, the beach barren as if we were the last, or first, people on earth.

There are no photographs of us from those days. During all my winter days with Cato in Calvados, it never occurred to me to bring a camera. If there were photographs of us, they would have been quiet ones of our routines, a new domesticity.

Ours were slow mornings, reluctant to leave the warmth of the bed. Afternoons were spent watching the water from one of the marina cafés, only the sound of native French around us, unlike the concerto of accents in Paris, or climbing the D-day tanks on the beach from where we watched the tide push in. Sometimes he went to see a doctor in the nearby city of Caen, while I wandered the cobblestone roads, peering in shop windows, waiting for him. Our early evenings, after darkness dropped, we took refuge by the fireplace, sharing pillows as we each read a book or one of us read to the other. Dinners, prepared and eaten together in the kitchen among candles and wine. Always eager for the day's end, the reward of a hot bath, clean bodies under the covers, where we'd sleep, then pull awake for another dose of each other, and drift into sleep again.

In the house by the sea, Cato and I slept together in a goose-feather cocoon, yet instead of finding tranquility in our shared bed, I dreamed intensely of my family. I dreamed of Santi and me as children, crouched on the floor picking fleas off a stray mutt we found behind our father's factory. We took the dog home, washed and deloused him, and christened him Rey. But he ran away a few weeks into his adoption and was hit by a car. Papi said some spirits are too wild to be kept—he'd tried to let us love him but he belonged to a wide-open world. It was the first death Santi and I experienced, and Santi still kept a photo of Rey beside his bed.

I dreamed of Beto during the first days of his arrival from the hospital when I still wished he were a girl. I'd longed for a sister, for our lost sister Eden to come back to us in the form of another child. Since learning of her existence I'd spoken to her in my mind, consulted her on problems as the older sister I felt I'd been meant to have. Santi and I watched over Beto in his crib, and I asked Santi if he would ever love the new baby as much as he loved me. He shook his head but it wasn't good enough. I made him promise, swear, cross his heart and hope to die, that he would never love Beto more than he loved me, and he promised. I always regretted being that manipulative, jealous child, because all these years later I suspected it was true; out of loyalty to me Santi had deprived Beto of his love.

I dreamed of my parents. These near-death dreams came in varied forms, always me with my parents, in a speeding car careening off a slick bridge, in a crashing airplane, in an unknown building surrounded by walls of fire. But each time, we survived, all of us, and I awoke, my hair damp around my face, saturated with relief.

Every night I felt Cato and I died a little—as if this growing closer was actually pulling us apart. I lay awake, his thin breath in my ear, feeling this communion was ending for no other reason than there is no beginning without an end, but I'd force myself back into slumber, press my eyes shut to black out the fear, and remind myself, *I'm still here. He is still here.*

I never told Cato of those dreams. I wanted to but part of me still feared scaring him off as if he were the feral boy Tarentina had compared him to months earlier, defaulting to silence and his primal burrowing into me at night, as if for body heat. I was afraid to overwhelm him with talk of all the people I belonged to and who belonged to me. He rarely volunteered anything about his father, except, when I asked about the blue cross on the kitchen wall. He told me it was made by his maternal grandfather, who'd been a silversmith and had lived in this house until his death when Cato was an infant.

"My mother grew up in this house, too," he said. "It belongs to me now. Not Antoine. For a time he pressured me to sell it. I told him he could disinherit me himself if he wanted, but this house will remain mine."

Antoine rarely visited anymore, preferring to make his appearances in the summer months, but he left messages for Cato on the answering machine, which he checked every few days. But if Cato called him back, it was when I wasn't around.

I don't know what I looked like in those days. I know what we were like as a pair, what he looked like to me, the image of him I beheld, but of myself, I only know who I was before and who I became after. I can't see my face. I know I was happy yet very scared, exhilarated, and I know my faces as such, but there is a fourth face, one I kept hidden from him, the eyes that knew, before understanding, what was to come, and I wonder if those eyes would have come across in a glossy still frame, under the right light, if either of us had bothered to take the picture. Perhaps it's just a trick of memory, remembering who we were while knowing what became of us.

11

After a month together by the sea, Cato's doctor told him that as long as he was cautious about what he exposed himself to, he would be strong enough to return to Paris with me. We stayed up late one night watching snow fall over the city in frosty chunks, covering tree branches, spreading over the garden in a marzipan sheet. In the morning, trains were delayed, busses stalled, businesses closed, the most dedicated commuters wrestled through four or five inches of pristine snow turning it into a slushy charcoal river. It was the perfect day to stay hidden, but Cato had run out of his medication, and because the pharmacy doors were all still shut on our block, he decided to go to his father's place for his spare inhaler. Curious, I decided to go with him.

I was surprised he didn't have his own key to his father's apartment. The butler opened the door to him, and I followed Cato down the corridor to his bedroom, ignoring his father's voice rattling through a phone call in another room. The machines were gone but it still looked as impersonal as a hotel room. I sat on the edge of the bed while he pulled a small box from one of the dresser drawers, went into the bathroom, and a few mechanical pumps and coughs later, returned to me with watery eyes, cheeks full of color, not the powdery complexion he'd woken up with in my arms that morning.

"Don't you want to say hello to your father while we're here?"

"He's busy. Another time."

But when we were nearly out the door, the old man called from behind us.

"Felix, why must you pass through this house like a ghost?"

I turned slowly and there he was, that stiff figure of a man feigning a smile, a mask of warmth, as his eyes fell on me beside his son.

"You don't stop to greet your father? What's become of your manners, my son?"

I thought they would at least hug, but they only shook hands like colleagues.

"Papa, this is Li—" Cato started to introduce us but his father interrupted.

"Yes, yes. How nice to see you again."

I smiled as he gave me his hand to shake as well. "Hello."

"Miss, would you mind excusing us so that I may speak to my son alone for a moment, yes?"

"You don't have to go if you don't want to," Cato muttered.

"Not a problem." I tried to sound as airy as possible. "I'll wait in the hall."

I heard a television in another apartment on the landing, dogs barking, a woman singing to herself in Spanish as she swept the marble floor in front of a doorway on the floor below. It was a melody I knew from my childhood. I went down a few stairs until I was on the same landing as the woman. She noticed me watching her and smiled.

"Excuse me," I said in Spanish, "what's that you're singing?"

"*Los Cisnes*," she said, and the song came back to me at once; *The Swans*.

"My mother sang that to my brothers and me when we were children," I said.

"Really? Such a sad song?"

"I never understood why she loved it so much, but she says when she left her country all she took with her were her songs."

"Where in Colombia are your parents from?" She could tell my accent was half a generation removed. I told her Bogotá and she told me she was from Tolima.

"Are you looking for work?" she asked, pointing to her doorway. "La Patrona is giving birth soon and needs a nurse. I only cook and clean these days. I'm too old to care for a baby."

"No, thank you." I didn't want to be rude.

"Maybe your mother will be interested?"

"She's in the States but thank you again for offering."

"So what are you doing around here?"

"I'm waiting for my boyfriend."

She watched me, suspicion spreading across her face.

"You're one of Antoine de Manou's girls, aren't you? That's where you just came from?"

But she didn't wait for me to answer.

"You should be ashamed of yourself. And you're stupid on top of it! Everyone knows those men have ways of making girls like you disappear. You're one in a million. One less of you and nobody will notice."

"No, you're mistaken," I tried, but she took one hand off her broom and approached me by the banister, grabbing my wrist.

"You're going to get yourself in trouble, girl. Now get out of here and don't let me see you around here again! Get out of here!"

I fled her yelling and went down the rest of the stairs to the courtyard, wondering what sort of girls she meant and what Antoine was up to with them.

When Cato came out to the courtyard a few minutes later and we started back toward the house, I said as cautiously as I could, "The maid on the floor below your father's place asked me if I was one of your fathers 'girls.'"

"Did she?" He was hardly impressed.

"What did she mean?"

"She was probably just looking for gossip."

I waited a few moments to see if he'd say more but he didn't.

"So, how did it go with your father?"

"Fine," he shrugged. "Normal, for him."

"He doesn't like that you're with me, does he?"

He looked up to the sky, then back to me, sighing. "Are you asking me for a lie?"

"Never."

"No, he doesn't like it. He's an old man with old ideas about the world. But I'm an adult. I do what I want. What he thinks doesn't matter to me."

I was unnerved by the idea that I'd precipitated some sort of quiet rebellion and felt pity for Antoine because, in spite of his bitterness, my Cato was not his Felix, yet his Felix was his only son and all he had.

I ran into Romain in the washroom sometime after two in the morning. We stood side by side talking to each other through the mirror as I scrubbed my face and he brushed his teeth with an inch of toothpaste on his finger. He was shirtless, wearing his black work pants low, the folds of his hip bones exposed. Giada was the one who told me he never wore underwear. He said he'd finished work late and had to open early for the lunch shift tomorrow and didn't feel like going all the way home to Gobelins for just a few hours. Tonight, he was crashing on Camila's floor.

"You haven't come by to read *Martin Eden* in a while."

"Oh, you miss me?" He pinched my arm. "It's okay if you miss me, Lita. You can admit it."

I rolled my eyes at him.

"I'm kidding. I've been busy and"—he pointed to Cato's shirt on me—"I know you've been busy, too."

I splashed my face with water while he put his mouth to the faucet, rinsed, and spit out onto the porcelain. I started back toward my room but Romain tugged my sleeve.

"Why don't you wait a bit?"

"Wait for what?"

"Keep me company while I smoke my last cigarette of the night."

I wrapped my bare legs in a towel and sat on the heater while Romain sat by my feet, took two cigarettes to his lips and lit them at once, before handing me mine. I couldn't stop myself from telling him about my encounter with the woman with the broom.

"So she thought you were a whore? So what? That's not a tragedy."

"It's not the first time it's happened in Paris," I said. "But I just can't shake the disgust on that lady's face."

"You want my opinion, Lita? You know I always have one."

"Let's hear it."

"Your problem is you take every bullshit moment as a defining event of your life. You let everything stick to you. You've got to learn to float, be above the tide, you know?"

"You're saying I should be more like you?"

"If you need a role model, feel free."

I took a few drags with him watching me.

"I have a question for you, Romain. Something I've been wondering about."

"I am at your service."

"How is it so easy for you to be with different girls all the time without feeling anything?"

"Who says I don't feel anything?"

"I just assumed."

"I feel things. I feel them then, in the moment, but when it passes, I let go."

"You don't get attached to the person?"

"Look, people are who they are whether I fuck them or not. Some I care for, some I don't."

"You don't think sleeping with someone is . . . intimate?"

He stared at me so long I almost regretted asking.

"Lita, I'm not fucking you right now but I think this moment between us can be considered what you, a girl who likes to label things, would call 'intimate.'"

"We're friends. It's different."

"Is it?"

There were footsteps in the hall. Romain and I automatically rubbed our cigarettes into the windowsill and flicked them out to the roof. By the time he shut the window Camila was in the doorway, wrapped in a pink silk robe puddling around her feet.

She didn't look that surprised to see us there but glared at Romain.

"I thought you said you were exhausted."

"I am. I'm just catching up with my friend here."

He leaned in and kissed me on each cheek before following her back to her room, leaving me alone on the heater. I waited a few minutes longer, studying my reflection in the windowpane, the same face, the same girl I'd always been, before crawling back into bed with Cato, who hadn't noticed I was gone.

12

My family had taken a two-bedroom suite, my brothers together in one room, my parents in the other, a living room between them.

"You can come stay with us for a few days if you want," my mother said after they'd pulled me into a chain of embraces and gotten the remarks about my pale face, dirty hair, and bad posture out of the way.

"If you want to get out of that house for a few days that's fine with us. It's comfortable here, mi amor. We have plenty of room."

I thought the best way around the suggestion was to ignore it. I turned my attention to Beto, who, wearing a natural smile, looked excited for the first time in years.

"I want you to show me Chateaubriand's park," he said, "and the Louvre, the obelisk, all the places you wrote me about."

"The park's just around the corner." I led him to the window. "You can probably see it from here." But we couldn't. Le Bon Marché and a few other buildings were in the way.

My father ordered room service, and we had a family breakfast in the sitting area while my brothers spread a city map out on the coffee table and my mother said in her quasi-apologetic way, "Don't feel obligated to entertain us, mi vida. We know you have your classes and studies to think about." But before her next breath she managed to add, "How's the kitchen in your house? What do you think about me coming over to cook dinner for you and all your friends?"

"You're on vacation, Mami," I said. "I don't want you to worry about cooking."

I made my way out of there as quickly as I could, telling them I'd be late for school, but Beto wouldn't let me go when I hugged him good-bye.

"You all should rest for now." I tried to sound like the voice of experience. "I'll come back later and we can spend the rest of the afternoon together."

They were quiet. All of them. And I couldn't leave them. Not for a lie, not to run back home into the haven of my bed with Cato.

Those early February days were the snowiest and sloppiest of any I'd know in France, with a whipping northern wind, but I would make sure my family—for all their skepticism—would love Paris as much as I did. I led them on the same tours Loic had invented for me during my first weeks in the city, all over Saint Germain, across the river through the Tuileries and Les Champs, through Montmartre and the Marais, the entire museum circuit, blistering gusts spitting in our faces, until they were near crying from exhaustion. By evening they were so tired, we'd never make it to any of the reservations the concierge made for my father, the foodie, and instead retired to their suite for room service or ate dinner in the hotel dining salon where Séraphine told me Nazis used to gather during the occupation.

And within those long bustling days, though separated by only a few street corners, the strands of my life seemed to grow further apart. My life in Paris fell away—there was no House of Stars, no friends wondering why I was taking so long to come home, not even Cato, who gave me the space to be with my family, entertaining himself out with Sharif or lounging around my room reading the collection of books I'd been amassing from Gallimard on Raspail. These were moments in which I felt uniquely possessed by familial joy, forgetting there was anything beyond this family sitting together in a hotel room, laughing together, teasing one another, as if we'd left our pressures behind back in the States and had once again displaced ourselves, a family of snails taking our house with us on our backs, all ties, all obligations—my father's business, my mother's network of assistance—left behind. And we were, at least for this week, our clan of five, free together, and we were all we needed.

But my family wanted to know the life I lived away from them. They wanted to see Séraphine's house, my bedroom, meet the people I lived with. I held them off for a few days. Séraphine was in with one of her doctors, so she couldn't receive my parents, but Loic came out to greet them, speaking wonders of me and how delighted the de la Roques were to have me under their roof. My mother produced a small box from her handbag, delicately wrapped with a card attached, a gift of a silver pillbox engraved with her name, for Séraphine.

I showed them around the house and gardens. Santi and Beto whispered that I lived in a dump, while my parents complimented the lovely architectural details, the elaborate (broken) moldings, the intricate Persian (hole-laden) rugs. I'd buried all of Cato's clothes in the back of my closet, and my room was as neat and clean for their arrival as it had ever been, but the photographs Naomi had taken of Cato and me together at Far Niente, and on a house outing to Chambord, remained tacked to the wall, and my parents and brothers noticed them, without comment. Since I'd told her about him, my mother had kept mum about Cato and never asked about him during any of our phone calls, as if she could will him away with her indifference.

Loic spread the word that my family was in the house. Maribel was at the studio, but Naomi and Saira quickly appeared on the landing just outside my room to introduce themselves. Dominique also came by, ever so polite, and Giada, fresh out of the shower, descended the stairs in nothing but a towel.

"How lovely to meet you all," my mother said and gave them each a hug.

I should have known the girls would flock to Santi. Camila was the first, but she was no match for Tarentina, who, upon seeing him, stared at me as if I were guilty of some terrible betrayal for hiding him this long. She met him with her expertly coy routine, and Santi, of course, never turned down gratuitous flirting.

My parents invited each of them to join us for dinner, and one by one, they graciously, thankfully, declined.

Except Cato, whom we finally found in the foyer as we were heading out. I hadn't expected they'd meet this way. I was still trying to invent the perfect scene for their first encounter, but here it was all at once: my family, the tall black-haired bunch surrounding Cato, pale and gaunt, his hair still uncombed from the morning.

"This is my friend Cato. He's in town for a while."

My mother's brows went up slightly but she didn't let on. All these days, not a mention of him from her side or mine.

My father shook his hand, every young man a nephew, a sort of son.

"I once knew a Gato Gonzales from Brooklyn. Any relation to you?"

"It's Cato, Papi," I corrected with a hard C sound.

"Is that Greek?" That was Santi.

"I don't really know," Cato said.

"It's a nickname," I was irritated. "We *all* have them."

"Short and sharp," my father took over. "Just the way I like it. My name is Alberto but I've only ever been called Beto with a B. Nice to meet you, hijo. Are you joining us for dinner?"

Papi called everyone hijo or hija but I could tell Cato was taken aback.

"Yes, sir. I'd like that very much. Thank you."

We took two taxis. I rode with Cato and my mother. She watched the city lights outside the window, not a sound between us but the faint hum of Radio Nova.

Cato cleared his throat, "Are you enjoying your time in Paris, Mrs. del Cielo?"

She didn't understand him the first time, with his accented English and her accented ear. I repeated the question in Spanish.

"It's beautiful." She sounded shy, little-girl-like, watching the building facades go by like a film.

The concierge sent us to some fancy place in the First, way too stuffy for our tastes, decorated in various tones of green, and nearly empty and overstaffed, which made the waiters all the more attentive.

"We should have taken them to Far Niente instead," I told Cato as we were quietly analyzing the menu around the large round table, the waiters watching us like bodyguards.

Beto leaned into my shoulder. "Is this guy supposed to be your boyfriend or something?"

I nodded, and he mumbled to Santi on his other side, "Affirmative."

Santi let out a low laugh that made everyone look up from their menu, and I knew everything was about to turn.

Their first tactic in exclusion was to speak only in Spanish, and when I interjected that we should stick to English tonight, Santi gave Cato a puzzled, "What? You don't speak Spanish? How is that possible?"

"He does," I said, "as well as you speak French," because Santi hated being reminded of what he wasn't good at.

My mother also kept to her mother tongue, but my father tried, as he would toward any friend of mine, to engage Cato in English, ask him about his studies, his work, what he did with his free time.

Cato told him how he lived on the coast and worked with boats at the marina.

"Hijo, would you believe I didn't see the ocean until I was twenty years old? And that was just from the plane. We didn't make it to a real beach until we took the kids to the Rockaways many years later. When I saw all that water, I thought I was in heaven."

"That's a beach in New York," I told Cato.

"Y esta muchchita, this one right here," my father pointed to me, "she hated the ocean when we first put her in the water. She hit the waves, smacked them, furious the water was touching her. She refused to even put her little feet on the sand."

Cato turned to me, amused. "You hated the beach?"

"I was a baby," I said. "Obviously I grew to love it."

And then Santi took over. "Did you know my sister almost got married? It wasn't even that long ago."

"That's not true," I said.

"I was sure she was going to go through with it. They were so in love. Isn't that right, Beto?"

Beto, the traitor, nodded.

"I couldn't stand the guy back then but I kind of miss him now," Santi said trying to sound nostalgic. "Lita broke his heart. Devastated the guy. Practically ruined his life."

Our parents did nothing to stop their performance. Papi only looked a little bored by their banter and pulled a piece of bread from the basket. My mother stared back at me with surrender.

"Lita's always been a girl who can't be held down. She even refused to work in the family business . . . she has told you about our family business, hasn't she?"

Cato nodded, though I'd described it more like a family-owned grocery store and less like a multinational corporation.

"Always Lita with her big dreams, talking about being a diplomat, moving from country to country, tasting different cultures like they're a slice of cake."

"Would you cut it out?"

"This is a free country, isn't it?" Santi laughed. "I mean, we all know France is full of neo-fascists, but a guy like me can still speak his mind, no? No offense to you, Gato, my friend."

"It's Cato," I said sharply. "Get it right."

The waiters appeared with the first course. I watched Cato face his soup, wish bon appétit to the table, though my brothers had already started eating.

The rest of the meal followed the same pattern. During dessert, when my father looked at me from across the table and told me I looked more like my mother than ever—his way of saying pretty—Santi reminded everyone of how I was often mistaken for a boy until I was about ten years old. Santi also pointed out that even though I'd skipped two years of school—second and fifth grade, which he said were no big deal because they were just "filler" years—I'd still never managed to be first in my class like he always was. And when he wasn't taking direct aim at me, Santi, with the help of Beto, guided the dinner conversation out of Cato's reach to home, and to people he did not know.

When it was over, we split into two taxis again. This time Cato and I rode with my father. Cato thanked him for dinner, and we dropped him on the corner of rue de Bellechasse so it would appear he was staying elsewhere.

"Let us know if you come to the States one day," Papi told him as he stepped out of the cab onto the sidewalk. "We'd love to have you over to our home. You ever been to the U.S.?"

"No, sir. Never."

"No? Well, you'll have to put that on your list. Things to do before you die."

My father held my hand across the leather seat as we continued back to the House of Stars. "Parece un buen muchacho, tu amigo. Kind of quiet. But a good handshake."

We were quiet the rest of the way until the taxi pulled up in front of the house and my father, as we pulled apart from our hug good night, said in a heavy tone so it came off more like an order than advice, "Mi amor, watch yourself."

"I always do, Papi."

"No, corazón," he shook his head, "I mean really watch yourself."

Cato arrived a short while later. I was already under the duvet. He pulled off his sweater, kicked off his shoes, and dropped into bed beside me. I wanted to apologize for the night, but how could I apologize for my own family? It felt like a betrayal.

He wrapped me into his arms from behind, pushed in close, and we lay quietly until he finally said, "Your parents are very nice. Your brothers seem nice, too."

I breathed. I told myself they weren't so bad. An average family. Certainly no worse than his father.

"It must feel good to have siblings. Having someone, in your case two, to share everything with. It must make a lot of things easier. I can't imagine it."

I was silent. It seemed he wanted to say more but was stopping himself. After a while he said, "You look so much like your mother, like she had you alone."

"I'm sure my father had something to do with it."

"I wish I could see that house you grew up in. With all the people and animals."

"You will. One day. Maybe in the summer you could come back with me."

"I haven't been on a plane since I was a child."

"No?"

"I've been on helicopters with my father. But no more planes. After I got sick the doctors said it would be too much of a risk with my lungs."

And then, as if he were talking only to himself, "I always thought life is long. I'll have time for all the things I wish I could do. But I turn around and ten years have disappeared, as if they never were at all."

"There's time," I said. "There is always time." But I wasn't sure what we were talking about anymore.

"Do you still want to do all those things your brother said you wanted to do?"

I nodded. "In a different way. But I still have big dreams."

"What are they?"

"To see the world. To do something meaningful."

"Promise you'll do those things. With me or without me."

"I promise. But you have to promise the same."

"I already know I can't do everything I wish I could do."

"You can do anything you want." Those were words I'd been raised on, but when I said them to Cato, I knew he didn't believe me.

We were quiet together for a long time before we fell asleep. That night I dreamed of his house by the sea, and in the morning when we woke I told him that as soon as my family was gone, I wanted to go back there with him.

Tarentina said Santi couldn't leave without experiencing a proper night out in Paris. She enlisted most of the girls, and even Loic and Rachid, but Cato stayed back at the house. I was convinced we were having fun. My brother was the center of attention, just as he was accustomed to being, but once he was hopped up on vodka, he went right for the probe, grabbing my elbow, shouting in my ear under the thundering nightclub bass that I was wasting my time with Cato.

I'd spent the day with my family. The snow had cleared, sun had broken through, and it was unusually warm. We'd walked through the Luxembourg Gardens, visited the catacombs and the miracle church, where my mother dragged Beto down to his knees at the altar. I said a few prayers of my own, mostly of gratitude. My brothers hadn't said another word about Cato and I'd forgiven them, even decided their possessive behavior had been kind of cute.

But it was just like Santi to wait until all was forgiven to ambush me.

Tarentina was on his other arm trying to pull him from the table to the dance floor, but he shook her off gently and stayed firm at my side.

"What are you going to do? Pack him up and bring him home with you? You two have nothing in common besides your puppy eyes for each other. That's not enough to get you to the fucking corner."

I tried to ignore him but Santi rotated me by the shoulders to face him.

"You're forgetting who you are, Lita. Let me remind you our parents took their first ride on an airplane as guests of a pair of dogs."

"You don't need to remind me of that."

"Oh, I do. I see that you think you're like your fancy friends now. This is *their* world. You, hermanita, are just passing through. And everyone knows it but you."

"This," he motioned to the club, the crowd around us, "this is not your life. This country is not your maldito country. That decaying blueblood tenement you're living in is not your home. *We* are your home."

13

With my family departed, we'd planned to go to Calvados for the weekend. Our bags were packed. Rather, one bag was packed with both our things. I took pride in that detail as I stood over the bed, folding his clothes with mine, accommodating our things the way we'd made room for each other in our lives and learned to fit together. He spoke from behind me, said my name in a tone I'd never heard from him, even and unfeeling, full of stillness as if he were alone in the room and practicing a line, not speaking it to me.

"Lita. I think I should go home alone."

I waited a moment before turning around to face him.

"What did you say?"

"I think I should be alone at my house for a while. And I think you should stay here."

There was a new remoteness in his gaze.

"I think . . . I think it's the best thing for us."

I responded by pulling my clothes from his, placing them on the bed beside the bag. There was less to unpack than I thought.

When I was through, he touched my arm. "Maybe you can come next weekend."

"It sounds like you don't want me there."

"It's not that I don't want you there . . ." There was burden in his voice.

I sat down beside my little pile.

"I thought you were happy all this time."

"I was. I am."

"Don't say we'll see each other again if that's not what you want."

"It's not that I don't want to see you, Lita."

"Then what is it?"

"I just think it will be easier if we stop things now."

"Easier than what?" I hated the scorn in my voice.

Cato shuffled his feet against the rug and let out a long sigh.

"We don't talk about it, but you know you're going to leave in a few months. And you know I can't go with you. We're just prolonging things."

"I wasn't as sure about my leaving as you seem to be."

"I just want to do the logical thing."

"Why is that?"

"Don't make me say it."

"You're going to have to because I don't know what you mean."

"Lita, we don't make sense. Anybody can see that about us." But the voice I heard was not his. It could have belonged to my brother, his father, Séraphine, or any of the girls in the house, but I knew it did not originate with him.

"Walk away then," I said coolly, with too much pride to show I was crumbling. "Leave right now if that's what makes sense to you."

To my surprise, he did.

Of course I cried. Until my eyes swelled and my face ached. In English the word for crying feels trite, empty. The Spanish llorando is so much better. To say it feels like a cry, the way you have to open up your mouth and throat, concluding on the tip of the tongue, the back of the teeth. The French pleurer sounds too pretty, restrained, a costume of sadness.

I wanted to invent a new word for crying without tears. That broken feeling. The disillusion.

On the third day, I finally opened the door to Tarentina. She pulled me out of my bed and into her arms, wiped my face clean, brushed my hair, and told me, in her Tarentina way of talking about love like a clinician, that men are capable of astonishing tenderness without feeling a single ounce of love, and those who do feel love usually don't have the faintest idea how to express it.

"I saw this coming, Lita, but I didn't want to spoil your fun. Had you asked for my advice I would have told you to withhold your affections a bit. Not be so available, serving yourself up like an apple-mouthed roasted pig. Men can take only so much beauty before they run. They're not women, you know."

"So it's my fault? I'm the one who failed?"

"No, of course not. He's right. You two don't make sense. But look at the bright side. You got what you came to Paris for, no?"

Tarentina's theory was that parents sent their daughters to Europe not to be educated but to get the thirst for love affairs out of their system so they can return home exhausted and disheartened enough to slip into the roles outlined for them since birth. She said a daughter is a father's primary investment, and all of us, except her, because she was fatherless, were a bunch of clipped-wing canaries. Sooner or later each of us would return home to our safe small lives, marry the boy who'd been picked out for us, and relegate memories of our Paris days to a quiet trove of photographs and diaries hidden in the back of a closet.

"None of the relationships in this house would ever translate to real life," she said. "These love affairs can only exist *here*. At the end of each séjour there are always tears and heavy promises, but there comes a time when every girl does as she's told, packs up her things, returns home, and leaves that lover behind. You'd have done the same, darling. Trust me. Count yourself lucky that your Cato said good bye before you had to. You'll have less regret that way."

I started to tell her I wasn't like other girls and Cato wasn't like other boys, but she held up her palm and told me in a voice that was both soft and severe, "I know you think you're special. You've probably been told you were special all your life. But there's a Lita in the House of Stars every year."

Séraphine sent for me. I curled into the violet armchair next to her bed and helped myself to one of her Dunhills. I waited for her to bait me for a confession but she only watched me, nodding her head with her slight, twitchy pulses. I looked around at the photographs lining the walls, a way for her to see her whole life in a tapestry every day. I used to think I wanted to be that way when I was old, surrounded by objects and artifacts from a life lived passionately and well, but now it seemed tragic: Séraphine, painted and immobile in her white bed mound, while the world danced on outside her doors. Somehow, I resented her at that moment.

"You must be thrilled your prediction came true," I said.

"Prediction?"

"You said he would leave me and you were right."

"Cynicism is an addictive pill, chérie. It doesn't suit you." She took a cigarette for herself, the lighter flame wobbling in her shaky hands. "Some people are gifted with love and don't know what to do with it. They're simply born to be alone. Love will always slip through their fingers like water."

"Am I one of those people?"

I stood up and walked to the window; spikes of winter air vibrated against the glass. Across the garden, the stone bench where I'd sat with Cato the night of the first party was covered with broken twigs and bird shit.

"No," Séraphine said, "you never will be. You love fully. I saw this much in you. But it's not love if you depend on a man to hold you up like a pillar. A woman must have roots in the earth, not wait for her lover to plant her in a beautiful clay pot. Yours was an honest mistake, chérie. If you had found a potent love earlier in life like some girls do at the age of thirteen or fourteen, you would be a very different woman."

"I was in love once."

"Were you?"

"I thought I was."

"Well, then you should know young love is not meant to last. It's just a glimmer that sets fire to a heart that will be repeatedly baptized with sorrows and abandonments until you arrive at the *right* love, which might not even be a love but more like a partnership, two people who fall into each other's lives in a way that is comfortable and inevitable."

"That doesn't sound very romantic."

"It's not mean to be, chérie. In the end we all become closer to who we started out as in life than who we set out to be. The best thing one can do is accept the life that was claimed for you the second you were born. Dreaming is for children. And one day, after everything, you will wake up and realize you really haven't suffered much at all."

* * *

I began walking the city trying to undo every step I'd taken with him at my side. I squinted against beastly white winter winds blowing off the Seine, walked along the quai all the way across to Place des Victoires, where I sat on the same curb to adjust the same leather boots I wore on our first outing.

I passed through the passages of the Palais Royal, stopping at the precise spot where he fell ill, remembering the shadows of his body on the pavement.

There were no brides and grooms posing for wedding photos beside the obelisk that day. No candied white gowns, tuxedos, or rose bouquets shedding petals in the street.

On the Pont Alexandre, a Russian family asked me to take their picture. The parents hugged the children as they stood along the wall in front of one of the lanterns. When they left, I went to the statue where we'd stood together the day the rain came down. I found our names on the bronze covered by more recent signatures. A piece of us remained.

I crossed Les Invalides up the boulevard to the Rodin Museum, passed through the galleries feeling more like a phantom than a person, out to the back garden, then moved slowly along the pebble paths watching lovers on the stone benches nuzzling each other, the sky darkening above. Before my tour was over I stopped in Chateaubriand's park to find it vacant, free of children and the usual elderly ladies hunched over needlepoint, the solitary old men smoking cigarettes and staring up at the clouds as if they held some secret. I sat on my bench, where I came that first day to write postcards to my brother, staring across the path to where he'd once sat and watched me. I could see him, sitting, one leg crossed over another. His slanted shoulders, sheepish smile. The mussed hair, pearly skin. I heard his voice. Heard him say my name.

*   *   *

Paris is a city of sidewalk love scenes any day of the year but on one February day, lovers become especially brazen, warmed over by some nuclear love bomb. You can't walk two meters without witnessing a meeting of tongues, bodies wrapped so far into each other that it's unclear where one ends and the other begins. In doorways, a guy standing before a girl with a bouquet in hand, anticipation all over his lips.

Tarentina and I were the only dateless Valentine refugees in the house. In her case it was by choice because she rejected displays of sentimentality. I wanted to stay home locked in the cavern of my bedroom, replaying every conversation I'd had with Cato to myself, searching the pauses, hesitations, and ellipses for clues that he'd had a foot out the door, but she forced me out with her that night.

She called Romain and asked him to hold us a table at Far Niente even though I hadn't opened the door for him when he came by a few days earlier to read *Martin Eden*, because I suspected he'd greet me with some sort of lecture. The House of Stars rumors were never restricted to only our walls, and the Far Niente waiters all knew Cato had split on me. Romain positioned my chair so my back was to the room full of couples, but when the violinist the boss had hired for the night began to play the opening bars of "Speak Softly Love," Tarentina ordered Romain to get the vino flowing.

Around midnight I went to the ladies' room and took a long look at myself in the mirror. I usually avoided mirrors. My mother would scold me for looking at my reflection too long as if she didn't want me to know myself too well. But this mirror in the tiny red bathroom of Far Niente seduced me into its shiny metal frame. I stared at myself, noticing new lines around my eyes and lips, my pasty complexion, my eyes droopier than I'd ever realized and, tonight, puffed like profiteroles with pink and purple fatigue marks pressed into the corners. I wondered if this was the same face Cato saw when he lay across from me in bed, when he kissed me.

I didn't know my face anymore and was unsure that I'd ever known it. During those months I thought it was enough to see myself through his eyes. I thought he saw someone special, beautiful, worthy of love. En route to the restaurant I'd felt the pavement belonged to him, stretches of rue du Bac he'd already claimed with me or on his way to me. The inky sky above was his, and now I felt an imposter in his country, each hour borrowed against hope that he'd reappear.

Someone knocked on the bathroom door. I said I'd be out in a minute, and when I opened it there was Romain looking ravenous, blocking me so that I couldn't step out past him but he could step in. There the kisses began. I don't remember the first one, just the succession that followed, the sloppy mouths finding each other, my disorientation as I forgot where I was, opening my eyes to an inch of myself reflected in the mirror, my face obscured by his curls, my body shrinking within his. It may have been seconds or minutes—I couldn't determine—before I stopped him as he started to unbutton my blouse. He didn't resist, seeming pleased to have gotten this far. We faced each other. His palms rested on my hips while I folded my arms against my chest.

Back at the table I drank more wine. Tarentina didn't let on that she noticed my flushed face or swollen lips. She was talking about Loic, how he'd fallen for a Jamaican ballerina named Corinne who'd come by the house asking if there were any open rooms for rent. She'd just been kicked out of the apartment she shared with her boyfriend on rue de Passy and heard about the House of Stars from a friend of a friend. Loic took her number and helped her find a chambre de bonne on rue Vaugirard through one of his contacts and, miserly as he was, had reserved a table at La Tour d'Argent to take her for a Valentine's dinner.

It was late. I told Tarentina I wanted to go home. We were the last people in the restaurant. Even the toothless homeless man had already come for his meal and gone. Romain had changed out of his apron and black shirt into his regular clothes. When he saw us get up to leave I could tell he was just waiting for the invitation. I looked at him and he looked at me and Tarentina pretended to look away. We walked out the door and he followed. Tarentina kept a few steps ahead and Romain walked beside me, his fingers gliding against mine, trying to find a place within them, but I kept pulling them away. Maybe it was the cocktail of wine and woe, the stench of romance rising from the concrete. I should have told him to leave that night but couldn't. I didn't want to be alone.

When we were in my bedroom and Tarentina had closed the door to hers, I told him he could stay the night if he wanted. He could even sleep in my bed, but we would *only* sleep. As I said the words I believed them, and by the way he stared at me, nodding, I thought he believed me, too.

I can't remember what his kisses felt like because I was numb, or my lips were, maybe from all the alcohol. I only remember that I wondered, with his body over me, trying to push my thighs apart with his knees while I resisted and kept them sealed, if I could make him my surrogate for the body I really longed for that night. I wanted to touch him, but my arms were heavy, so I lay limp, trying to respond with my lips, hoping that kissing him would keep the room from spinning, but after a few minutes I couldn't take it anymore, pushed him off me, and ran down the hall to the bathroom to vomit.

When I came back to my room, Romain was on the floor, using his shirt as a pillow. I stepped over him to get back into my bed and was just beginning to fall asleep when I heard him whisper, either to me or to himself, "We always want the ones who don't want us."

14

I met Pascal one night when Tarentina took me to a private party at the Musician's place. Pascal was a stringy blond and sat next to me on a purple velvet sofa after Tarentina disappeared to one of the bedrooms with the Musician, leaving me in a room full of strangers. It was the first time I'd seen the Musician in person, and it was hard to separate the man from the stories I'd been told about him. How he'd been inviting Tarentina to join him on tour since she was seventeen and showered her with vacations and gifts. The songs he'd written, including one about a Brazilian orphan girl that went on to become one of the biggest hits of his career. Yet she claimed he was a sad man, and alone in his room he looked much older than his fifty-five years with a sunken chest and rodent-like curve to his back that he concealed with gypsy blouses, leather jackets, and long robes. She swore their relationship didn't involve much sex, maybe because of his age or because he got enough of it elsewhere, but something kept him hooked on Tarentina. She said everyone else hassled him too much, always asking for money or favors, not just the industry people but his family back in his Belgravia mansion, and when it was just the two of them, he was happy to let Tarentina be the star.

One of the Musician's regular guests, Tarentina had pointed out, was Dominique's father, a bloated, graying goateed man with his hands on the hips of a young miniskirted model, and that was the reason she never brought the other girls along with her to these parties no matter how much they begged for an invitation.

Pascal only went by his first name and was a singer-songwriter and protégé of the Musician, discovered while performing for change in the Charing Cross tube station in London. Pascal inched his way over from his end of the sofa and offered me a cigarette—Chesterfields—trying the line on me that I looked like one of Gauguin's Tahitian girls, which I ignored, and instead pulled out my own pack of smokes, but Pascal was undeterred.

He said I had the face of a stranger, and he was a stranger, too. Though he could easily pass for continental French he was actually a Caribbean boy, the son of a fifth-generation Martiniquaise, raised in Margot until sent at sixteen to finish school in Limoges.

"And what are *you* doing in Paris?" he asked me.

He was a good-looking, well-styled vagabond, in torn jeans and silver rings on too many knuckles.

"I'm in school," I lied, because it was easier than explaining that I'd dropped out and my only work was running a term-paper mill, though it paid for the new dress and high-heel leather boots I was wearing that night, as well as the lace bra and panties Tarentina convinced me to buy at Sabbia Rosa because she said my clothes were so dull she couldn't stand to wonder what I wore underneath.

"I'm at the Sorbonne." And that was only a relative fib because some afternoons I crashed lectures there since they didn't take attendance or check IDs. It was part of my recent plan of self-education. I knew my months in Paris were coming to a close, so

I'd assigned myself a list of cultural excursions, from the Chapelle Expiatoire to the Cimetière des Chiens, Rouen, and the Loire. But nights were still a lonely matter, so I accepted almost any invitation that came to me, falling into Giada's crowd of party people, following her favorite DJs from club to club or on a blind double date with a pair of Oliviers who took us to that fondue place in Montmartre where they serve wine in baby bottles.

Sometimes the couples took me into their care. Saira and Stef invited me to dinner and to the movies with them, and Naomi dragged me along to Rachid's boxing matches in Aubervilliers and Clichy-sous-Bois. But nights out with Tarentina were always the biggest production, with her two hours of primping that included music, stretches, and the practicing of smiles, pouts, and scowls in the mirror because, she said, the easiest way to seduce a man is make him a little afraid of you.

"With the right glance, you can make a man doubt every choice he's made in his life and make him yours for as long as you want him."

And maybe she was right because the more I behaved indifferently to Pascal, the more he seemed to care about impressing me.

Tarentina stayed with the Musician that night and Pascal offered to drive me home.

"I've been here before, years ago," he said when he pulled his Citroën up to our green doors. "I came to a few parties here. It's called the Dollhouse or something, no?"

"The House of Stars."

"Right, right."

I didn't look at him until I was out of the car, thanking him for the ride. I felt foolish. I didn't know how to handle these sorts of moments.

Tarentina agreed that I needed guidance. She arranged for us to run into each other a few more times, at nightclubs and bars, when I realized I'd been paired off with him, and she with the Musician. Pascal was full of plans, telling me in detail about the album he was recording with the Musician as producer, performing in local showcases, planning a tour in Japan that fall after a two-month retreat to his favorite ashram in Rajasthan. He was a "Nowhere Man," as the girls called such rootless wanderers. He'd spent years traveling in South America with his guitar on his back, and even passed through my namesake, Leticia. Tarentina believed he was the antidote to Cato, bound to his little cottage by the sea. I made an effort to like Pascal, who, for some reason, treated me as if I fascinated him. But as we sat around a tiny table at Castel's one night, I complained to Tarentina that I felt entirely absent, a mere prop of a girl.

"That's part of the process, darling," she told me. "You have to train yourself to be with another man. Everyone does it. You'll get used to it."

I invited Pascal to Florian's gallery reception for the unveiling of Maribel's painting, as yet *Untitled*. Every year he picked one student to show their work alongside his, and this time she received the honor, though it wasn't free of rumors about their affair and favoritism because of her parents' fame. When we all arrived for the reception, she led us around the gallery, past Florian's paintings to the far wall where her piece hung under a row of track lights, an amalgam of dark tones stippled with paler tinges, shapeless forms woven together that didn't follow any logic I could identify. Maribel said logic was the enemy of creation and a painting should never be literal, because our minds and souls are not literal.

"So I guess you won't explain it to us then?" Camila asked on behalf of our cluster, but Maribel scoffed that an artist should never be asked to explain. To explain is to justify and to justify means one fears judgment, and doubt alone will destroy any chance a work has of being authentic.

The others moved on to look at Florian's paintings, and Pascal and I stopped by the bar. We took our wineglasses to a corner of the gallery, and he brushed a runaway strand of hair from my face, the intimacy of his gesture startling me, which I think he noticed because he pulled back and slipped his hand in his pocket.

We formed a little wall, speaking of the others, observing them together. Across the gallery Florian held court over a crowd of art folk, while photographers flashed away. He and Maribel avoided each other, while Eliza fluttered about the room; an ever-tan song of a woman who I heard left two children behind in Tarragona years ago to be with Florian in France. That made me curious about her. I wondered to what degree a woman had to love a man in order to leave her children and country for him. Maybe it was like Séraphine once said: The reason the end of love, the severing of intimacy, what in Spanish we call desamor, is so painful is that romantic love is but a cult of one.

That and that each of us gambles our life on what we believe to be the truth.

I thought of the night I was introduced to Florian, how I'd stood on the edge of his boat looking across the water at the lights on the other side of Paris.

And Cato, by the torch, out of the shadows and into the streetlights on the long walk home.

I tried to stop my thoughts, but in the gallery, no matter which way I turned for diversion, from the faces of the people, to the ambiguous artwork, and to Pascal next to me, waiting for some kind of signal that I was ready for him to kiss me, all thoughts led me back to Cato.

Pascal took my hand.

"Are you all right?"

"I need some air." It wasn't a dizzying sensation that came over me but a sudden clarity that I was in the wrong place.

We went out to the sidewalk. He lit a cigarette and leaned against the building while I stopped on the curb, looking to the darkened storefronts across the street. I saw a familiar body walk by in clinging black attire. I was sure it was Sharif, the midnight ninja out for a night tagging the city, and called his name but he didn't hear me.

"You know him?" Pascal was surprised but I was already crossing the street, following the guy down the opposite sidewalk, calling after him until he finally turned around and barked, "What do you want?" into my face.

"I'm sorry," I said and backed up right into Pascal. "I thought you were someone else."

"Lita." Pascal put an arm around me and led me back to the gallery. "Why don't we get out of here? We can go to my place, or yours if you want."

His arm was still around me as we sat in the back of the taxi, yet everything about the night felt wrong, and it was only when we arrived at the House of Stars and faced each other on the sidewalk, when he told the taxi driver to keep the meter running, before giving me a single kiss on the cheek and telling me with a blend of kindness and restraint to "take care," that I knew Pascal felt it, too.

And then I saw it. The form of a man's body sitting in the shadows of the stone steps. Loic and Gaspard were still at the gallery. It was someone else.

I stopped walking, halfway across the entrance court.

He leaned into the stream of moonlight.

Cato.

I'd stopped hoping for a moment like this, and now that it was here, I tried to muster indifference, so he wouldn't see that despite two months of silence, I only wanted to run to him.

"Don't tell me you're lost."

"No. I'm waiting for someone."

"The others are all at Maribel's show in the Marais."

I stopped just short of the stairs where he sat.

"I didn't come here for any of them."

"Who did you come here for then?"

"I came to see you."

"Well, here I am." I started up the steps toward the door but he caught my hand.

"Lita, sit with me a minute. Please."

I took a deep breath, as if that would give me fuel, and sat a palm's width from him, wanting to close my eyes and forget he left that day—rip myself away from this moment, where we sat as new strangers.

"What is it you need to say?" It was easier to keep my eyes to the ground.

"I've been wanting to tell you . . . I tried to pretend we never met."

Me too, I wanted to say, but only because he'd given me no other choice.

"I thought it would be easier if I left you to be free to have fun with your friends, enjoy the rest of your time in Paris without being stuck with me."

"I never felt stuck with you."

"I've been alone so long. It's the only way I know how to be," he spoke to the wind in a near whisper, steady and slow as if he'd practiced what he'd say.

"I know you came to see me when I was sick. And then one day you were gone."

"Your father told me not to come back."

"I know."

"And it was Christmas. I went to see my family. I came to see you as soon as I returned. Don't you remember?"

"Yes, yes. But that's what I'm trying to tell you. Everything that matters to you is in another country. No matter what, this is going to end with one of us leaving the other."

"You mean me."

"It has to be you. I'll always be here."

"You talk like you're sentenced to the life you have."

"I don't have the freedom you have. My body isn't strong enough to jump around the world like you can."

"What if I stayed?"

Cato met my eyes, just as surprised as I was by my words.

"If you stayed, it would be . . . different."

We were quiet until the space shrank between us and I felt his side against mine, his arm reaching around me.

"Cato, what did you come here for?"

"I came for you." His breath warmed my cheek when he spoke.

"Are you sure that's what you want?"

"*You* are what I want. I'll take however many days we have left together, if you'll take me."

And like that, it was undone, and we were restored, or so I believed.

Cato departed again a week later, this time with me at his side on the morning train back to the house by the sea. We opened the windows and cleaned together, making it ours again. I went with him to look in on some of the boats he took care of, bobbing like tops in the harbor. I liked watching him. There on the boat deck he was strong. He pulled heavy levers and hooks, hauled piles, and pushed loads with no indication he'd ever been weakened by sickness. Here, he was a magician, the wind roping through his hair, handling a piece of engineering, and with a flick of his hand the sail went up, swift like a handkerchief.

One afternoon Cato prepared the vegetables left at the door by the lady from down the road, and I took the bicycle to the marina to get the fish for dinner from a friendlier fisherman I'd discovered farther down the docks—a Brit from Dover who'd made the crossing for a woman in Honfleur he'd met and married through an ad. I pedaled down the muddy trail easily, as if I'd done so all my life.

This life with him, the marriage of the landscape with our new routines, seemed paradisiacal to me. It didn't even bother me that in his village people still stared at me when Cato and I walked around together holding hands as if I'd taken one of their own hostage.

That day, I thought I could get used to Cato's small town.

I believed I could live there. If only he would ask me.

And then he did.

We lay on the floor of the room in his house with the books, though this time, the fireplace was cool and empty. There was no music, only the first sounds of spring, birds outside the window.

"If you wanted," he started carefully, "instead of going home this summer, you could stay in France longer. In Paris. Or . . . you could stay here . . . with me."

I wanted him to be sure of what he was asking, and he must have known, because he offered something of a plan.

"You could find a job here easily with your English, or you could study at the university. Not forever. I know you have other plans for your life. But for a while longer. For as long as you like."

I was relieved to hear he wanted me beyond the expiration of my carte de séjour. Though if I didn't officially maintain a student visa, I'd have to leave and return as a visitor, or stay on, illegally.

I watched him sleep easily that night in his own bed, searching the shadows of the room for a sign, a rune cast in the moonlight over the chipping paint of the walls. I tried to envision a new life. I could find work translating, teaching English, or tutoring. I figured the countryside might be less competitive than Paris and already knew I could find plenty of work writing academic papers for lazy students. I could look after somebody's kids. I could take up another degree in some kind of French history at the Université de Caen, like he said.

But to go anywhere, to begin again, one must leave something behind.

My family. My home.

He pulled me close.

"I love you, Lita."

He said it first in French, then English, and Spanish, and the words pushed deeper, but I stopped him, "Don't say that," because it didn't matter the language; they weren't the words I wanted.

"What should I say then?"

"Don't say you love me. Say you choose me."

"I choose you."

"And say it again every day."

When we returned to Paris we found an ambulance parked inside the courtyard, the front doors to the House of Stars wide open with a group of paramedics standing around the foyer while the other girls arranged themselves on the stairs to take in the show below. Cato and I took a place among them.

Earlier that night, as Violeta helped her get ready for bed, Séraphine had fainted, sliding off her mattress onto the floor. By the time the medics arrived, she was lucid and forbade them to take her to the hospital. The ambulance workers stood around waiting for a decision to be made while Loic and Gaspard tried to convince their grandmother to let herself be examined, but all the girls heard was her howling echo against the marble of the foyer.

"Leave me in my house! Leave me!"

Loic appeared, a hand on his temple.

"She won't go. She absolutely refuses."

As if she heard him, Séraphine shouted from her room, "I will not leave my house! Leave me in my house!"

"At least we know she's not short of breath," Tarentina offered, but the medics ignored her and warned Loic she needed to be seen by specialists, not just the doctors that came for house calls and to deliver prescriptions.

Loic and Gaspard looked at each other. It was the first time I saw any shred of fraternal union between them.

"I'm sorry to waste your time," Gaspard said. "There's nothing to be done. She won't let herself be taken from her house."

When they'd cleared out, Tarentina asked if we could go in and see Séraphine while Cato waited in the foyer with the other guys.

That night we saw Séraphine free of artifice, in her eyelet nightgown, face wiped clean of her lotions, tints, and pigments, just the vague outline of kohl liner. Her long white hair was brushed smooth, parted in the middle, falling to her elbows, though the fat bun she often wore turned out to be a hairpiece now lying in a neat bundle on her bedside table.

She pulled the blanket above her chest when she saw our cluster inch through her doorway.

"Don't tell me they've sent you all in here to try to convince me to go," she said.

"No, the medics have all left," Tarentina assured her. She went to Séraphine's side, holding her hand while the rest of us crowded around her bed. "We just want to make sure you're all right."

"My darling girls," she sighed, "nothing good comes from being old."

"Maybe you should consider going to the hospital sometime, not today, of course, so they can take a look at your heart," Giada tried.

"Why? To help me die faster?"

"They can do tests and find ways to make you more comfortable."

"Chérie, when people my age go to the hospital they don't come out."

She set her stare back on Tarentina, clutching her hand tighter and pulling it to her chest.

"I will die in this house." She closed her eyes.

"Don't talk like that." Tarentina lowered herself to sit on the bed at her side.

"This house is mine to die in. It's what I want."

"You still have many years ahead of you."

"Please, Chérie. Time forgives no one." She let go of Tarentina's hand and stared at the photographs on her walls as if they held answers, her eyes bluer than ever.

"Do you have any idea how many girls have passed through this house?"

We were all silent.

"I'll tell you. There have been hundreds of you. Hundreds." She reached for her cigarettes but thought better of it and dropped her silver case on the floor with resignation.

"Some girls stayed a few months. Some for a year or two or three." She looked at Tarentina. "Or *five*. You become my daughters. You become my heart. And when you leave do you know how many return to see me? Do you know how many write me a letter or offer me a phone call? Can you guess how many? In all my decades opening my house to you girls full of your passions and dreams, maybe two or three. To all the rest, I am forgotten."

"Séraph—" Tarentina started but Séraphine cut her off.

"My house will become a story you will tell your husbands and children and friends at dinner parties. My little birds, mark my words, you will soon leave me and you will forget me. But this is natural. It's to be expected. I have given you my house but my house belongs only to me. And no matter what anyone says, because they think I am an old woman and this gives them the right to tell me what to do, I will remain here in my house because it is my right and it is what I desire, until my last breath."

15

Cato presented the idea as his father's initiative.

"My father invited us to spend Easter Sunday with him."

"Are you sure he meant both of us?" I was incredulous.

"Yes, he asked specifically that you come. We'll join him for Mass first and go to his home afterward for lunch. What do you think?"

"I think that sounds . . . nice."

I'd spent every Easter of my life with my family, and here I was meeting Antoine on the steps of La Madeleine. We were late. It was difficult to come by a taxi on Easter morning and we had no choice but to take the métro—Cato's first time since I'd met him. He covered his mouth for most of the ride, tapping his foot and watching anxiously as the subway line chart counted each stop before we arrived.

"Haven't I always told you punctuality is a virtue?" Antoine said to his son.

He turned to me and shook my hand as if we were meeting for the first time.

"Please." He motioned to an usher waiting behind him, indicating that we should follow him down the aisle below the vaulted ceiling and painted domes to our reserved seats a few rows from the altar.

Afterward, we rode home with Antoine in his chauffeured car. His butler received us, and Antoine led us toward the sitting room with the framed military portraits where I'd waited on my first day visiting Cato. The butler offered us drinks but I only took water. He offered us hors d'oeuvres, too, but I was so nervous I declined. It's not that I was anxious to have Antoine's approval. It was more that I feared my relationship with Cato could fall prey to a game of loyalties.

At Séraphine's urging, I'd borrowed a pale gray spring suit from Tarentina. They'd both been as surprised as I was that he'd returned to me after so much time apart.

"You need to be impeccably dressed, chérie. This is *the* gesture. The old man is acknowledging your relationship. Either that or his son put him up to it."

I remembered the day Antoine warned me not to return to see Cato, and yet here we were, sitting together in his salon, me on the edge of the mauve sofa and Antoine leaning back into a blue armchair as Cato sat across the coffee table on an ottoman, both of us listening to his father talk about the weather.

"How lovely when Paris resurrects each April, don't you agree, Laura?"

"Leticia," Cato corrected.

"Ah yes, *Leticia*. Forgive me. And what is it you study here in France?"

Somehow, diplomacy didn't seem like the right thing to say, and I couldn't very well mention that I'd long ago stopped attending classes at the language institute.

Cato sensed my hesitation, stepping in with, "She studied international relations."

"Going into the foreign service, are you?"

"I'm more interested in the social aspects of transnationalism."

He didn't seem to care what my responses were, but about hitting all his points of inquiry.

"And tell me, Leticia, when is it that you'll be going back to . . . to . . . your country?" He turned to his son, "Where is it she comes from?"

"The United States," I answered for myself. "I'll be going back in June." That was, after all, still the date printed on my return ticket.

"That's quite soon." He seemed pleased.

The butler came in to tell us lunch was ready and we could take our seats in the dining room. Antoine sat at the head of the long table, with Cato to his right and me to his left. A second butler arrived to assist in serving an asparagus soup. When the main course of Lapin Rôti was set before us, I froze.

"Bon appétit," Antoine said, and he and Cato cut into theirs while I picked at the accompanying potatoes and spinach until there was nothing left but the meat and I had no choice but to put my fork and knife down.

The younger butler arrived at my side looking worried.

"Is there something wrong with your food, miss?"

"No, it's fine. I'm just not very hungry." I hoped that would be enough.

"You didn't even try it," Antoine remarked mid chew, bits of meat on his gums. "It's exquisite. You must have a taste. I insist."

"I'm sorry. I don't eat rabbit."

"Why not?"

"My family keeps them as pets."

I noticed Cato trying to hide a smile from across the table, but his father was not at all amused.

"Exactly how many rabbits do you have?"

"About thirty, the last time I counted."

"You keep thirty rabbits *inside* your home?" Antoine appeared revolted by the notion, staring at his son as if he'd brought some sort of lunatic to the table.

"They live in an enclosed atrium."

"And you allow them to keep reproducing, as if in the wild?"

"Most of them are neutered"—I had to ask Cato to translate the word *neutered*. "There might be a few more now. They're my brother's."

"We can ask the chef to prepare something else for you to eat instead," Cato said.

It was strange to hear the formal tone he acquired in his father's presence.

"No, thank you. I'm full already. The soup was delicious."

Over dessert of a custard tart, Antoine asked me who had recommended me to live in Séraphine's place. I told him how one of my teachers, a relative of Théophile's, had put us in touch and after I wrote a letter of introduction and filled out the forms, I'd been interviewed over the phone.

"It's a shame about Théophile," he said.

"It is. I've heard a lot about him. I would have liked to meet him."

"He was a kind man, from what I remember. Very sensitive, is what they say. He hanged himself in one of the top floor bedrooms. One of the grandchildren found him."

Cato and I were both in disbelief at hearing his father's recollections.

"I didn't know that," I managed, wondering if it had been Loic or Gaspard.

"As they say, every house has its secrets." Antoine sipped from his wineglass. Cato and I exchanged glances.

"I must say your French is quite good, Leticia. But you may want to consider taking elocution lessons. It would help the problem of your accent."

"How is it a problem?"

"It's certainly not terrible, but, how shall I put it? It is a bit distracting." I could tell he thought he was being complimentary.

"She already speaks several languages," Cato came to my defense. "A subtle accent is hardly anything to be concerned with."

"That's very unusual for an American. I assume you were nationalized."

"I didn't have to be. I was born there."

"How fortunate for your parents."

"I met Lita's parents when they came to Paris," Cato told his father. "They're very warm and gracious people."

"Is that so?"

"Yes."

"And tell, me Leticia, what is it your father does for a living?"

"He works in food distribution."

"Is that another way of saying he is a waiter?"

"It's another way of saying he owns the largest Latin American food manufacturing company in the world."

Antoine was quiet for a moment. He then moved the conversation to more neutral ground, complaining about the traffic and what he feared would be an imminent infrastructural collapse when all the fanatical soccer fans and tourists arrived for the World Cup that summer.

When Cato and I prepared to leave, I thanked his father for the invitation, and he took my hand, cupping it with his other.

"Perhaps we won't see each other again as you will be leaving France in the relative near future, but I do wish you well in your endeavors."

"She hasn't decided yet if she's leaving," Cato said, which surprised me. "She's considering extending her stay."

"I see." Antoine dropped my hand and took a slow step back. "Well, you will have to excuse me now, children. I've enjoyed your company but now I must rest. Leticia, please send my regards to Séraphine."

He turned his back to us and started down the hall to his study. Séraphine later forced me to write a note to Monsieur de Manou dictated by her, thanking him for his kindness and telling him how I'd so enjoyed the pleasure of being in his home.

On the walk home that Sunday, Cato and I tried to make light of the afternoon.

"Are you sure your mother didn't have an affair?" I teased. "Maybe he's not really your father."

"My mother was faithful to a fault," he laughed. "He's definitely my father."

After a few more steps, he added, "When you get to know him better you'll see he has some very good qualities."

"Like what?"

"To begin, he's extremely brilliant. Really, he's some kind of genius."

"I was taught it's not what you are that matters, it's what you *do* with it."

"I don't know if I believe that."

"What do you believe then?"

"I think all people are fundamentally good."

"So if I'm a saint in my own mind but a demon in the streets, what would that make me?"

"Are you calling my father a demon?"

"No, I'm saying it's our actions that define us."

"People are not only *one* thing all the time, Lita. He's just a man like I am just a man, and he's allowed to be complex and contradictory. There are many different sides to him. That's human nature."

"Not with my father. What you see is what you get."

I admit, maybe I sounded smug.

"Well, you're very lucky your father is so perfect, but Antoine is the only father I have."

I was quiet, regretting that I hadn't shut up sooner. Cato paused, too. When we were back on rue du Bac, the noise of the banging drums of a protest on the boulevard headed our way, Cato halted on the sidewalk, and met me with a desperate look I'd not seen on him before.

"Don't you think I wish I could change him? Don't you think all my life I haven't dreamed that he would wake up one day and just be *different*? I can't change him, Lita. He never changed for my mother and he is not going to change for you or for me."

"I'm sorry I—"

"Don't. Don't."

I was silent.

"I know how you feel," he said. "It's just the way things are. But I've forgiven him for the way he is even though he's never asked me to."

I thought of my own father. When I was a child I asked him if he ever forgave his father for having abandoned him in the park that day. He looked thoughtful and took his time before answering, "Mi amor, sometimes you have to let part of yourself die so that the rest of you can live."

A few days later Séraphine started calling each girl down to her room to ask if she planned on staying in the House of Stars another year or if she should make the room available to a new tenant at summer's end. When it was my turn at her bedside, I told her I didn't want to go home when the lease on my room was up.

"Well then, chérie, what do you want?"

"I want this life, here, not necessarily in the House of Stars, but I want the life of who I am today, going where I want when I want, doing what I desire. I want the chance to keep exploring."

"You don't want to leave your Cato, do you?"

I shook my head.

"Then stay."

"You don't understand how it is with my family. They'd die if I decided not to go home."

"I do understand. I was in your position once. Théo and I lived in Athens for one year in the sixties. He had business there and was very busy, and I met a marvelous Greek man and we spent several months as lovers. When it was time for Théo and me to return to Paris, the Greek asked me to stay in Athens with him. We planned that I would go to the airport with my husband but let him get on the plane without me. The Greek—I can't remember his name—waited in a car outside the airport. But at the moment my Théo reached for my hand and said, 'Séra, come, the plane is going to leave without us,' I could not help but follow him."

"You chose Théo."

"No. It was not Théo I chose, but the life that waited for me here, in Paris. I was born for this life, this house. It was my destiny. For a time I regretted how I left the Greek man, but now I think it's best to leave that way, without tears and embraces. Good-byes don't serve anyone."

"You think I should go home."

"Oh, Leticia, I don't have advice for you. I only have my stories. But if you *do* decide to stay, please remind your father to send a check for the deposit, yes?"

"You never heard from the Greek again?"

"Perhaps fifteen or twenty years later, I returned to Athens with Théo. We went to a restaurant in Plaka and I saw a man walking by a row of shops. He was the man I'd loved yet not the same man, tired, with wrinkles and a slow gait, and I understood love is not always what it appears to be. Love was not that stranger. Perhaps I even invented him. Love was the man at the table beside me, though sometimes we did not care much for each other. Love was my family name and my country."

She rubbed her cigarette into her ashtray.

"Come, chérie, come to my side." She made room for me on the mattress and took my hand in hers. "My dear Leticia. Sometimes the worst thing is bliss, because once you have experienced it, you know it is very unlikely you will find it again."

I stayed with her a while longer. We talked about other things. She told me she had decided that this summer she would make it out of the House of Stars and take a trip to Deauville, where she used to love to go for the parties and casinos with Théo.

"I'm going to die soon, and I don't want to leave this life without seeing the sea one last time."

"Don't say that."

"Why not?" She clutched my hand tighter. "Even a woman facing death can have a dream. And mine is to see the sea again. I have had a long and full life, chérie. I am now coming to the end of it. There is nothing wrong in saying so and telling those I care for that they should prepare for me to leave them soon. It's the truth. And we must love the truth even when it is the opposite of what we desire."

Those weren't her last words to me, but they're the ones I remember now.

She died that night.

They didn't want us in the house when they came to take her away. Loic said she wouldn't have wanted to be seen in such an unflattering light. She would want to be remembered as the woman she was the day before, not as the large body removed on a folding metal gurney by the muscles of four men from the funeral service company.

The funeral was only for family. We thought that included us, but Loic said it didn't. They buried her beside Théo in the de la Roque family plot near Chantilly. After the service, Loic and Gaspard returned to the house with their family, which included Séraphine's niece and nephew and their spouses, and an older woman I later learned was Loic and Gaspard's mother, Nicole. They went into the salon and closed the double doors behind them. Loic came out two or three times, calling for the maids to bring them fresh coffee and something to eat. Hours passed. A few of us gathered by the stairs on the second-floor landing, trying to guess what was going on.

The next morning the maids went around knocking on the bedroom doors summoning us to a meeting held over breakfast in the dining salon. At nine, all the girls were seated and present, though some of us were still in robes, while Loic and Gaspard sat side by side in two chairs at the head of the table. They looked almost like twins that day in their white button-down shirts and black trousers, their eyes worn with the same rings of weariness dipping down to their cheeks.

Gaspard put his palm to his brother's back as if to give him the strength to speak.

"I apologize. I haven't had much sleep." Loic cleared his throat. "Let me begin by saying I know you are all grieving as we are. The past few days have been difficult as you may imagine, but with the participation of other family members, we have come to some decisions. We hope you will find them agreeable."

"The House of Stars will remain open through the summer," Gaspard continued as if they'd been assigned their lines. "But we will close the house at the start of August, at which point we will begin liquidating its contents in preparation for it to be placed on the market in September."

"We're being evicted?" asked Tarentina, the designated spokesperson for our group.

"Believe me," Loics sounded regretful, "my brother and I would like nothing more than to keep the house open, but we are not the ones responsible for this decision."

"Who is?"

"Our mother."

Dominique uncovered the full story later. Nicole, with additional support from her cousins, who were due to inherit a small percentage of Séraphine's estate, decided to sell the house as Nicole had always wanted, promising her sons their share so they could each buy a small apartment. Loic and Gaspard had argued that the house was a treasure and they'd be fools to give it up. They said they'd assume responsibility for its upkeep and maintenance, if only the family was willing to hold on to it. They loved this house in a way none of the others did. But Nicole refused.

We got a good look at her the next day when she let herself into the house. She was an especially pale woman with a drinker's face, a kerchief of short blonde hair, with no feature in common with her mother beyond those de la Roque aquamarine eyes. She wore no makeup and was thin like her sons, dressed in ill-fitting navy pants and a white blouse with a Peter Pan collar that appeared on its fourth or fifth wearing without a wash. She was followed by the real-estate agent she'd appointed to find a buyer.

"The house needs a lot of work," I heard her tell him as they walked through the grand salon, "but I insist it be sold as is."

She led him upstairs and knocked on each of our doors to show the man our bedrooms, pointing to walls that could be knocked down to create larger rooms. She never introduced herself or asked our names. Cato and I waited silently by my doorway as she stood in the middle of my room telling the man, "The house will of course be much easier to show once the tenants have cleared out all their belongings."

And then she received a call on her mobile phone.

"I'm just finishing up some business here," she told the caller in near-perfect English. "You wouldn't believe the headache it's been. I'm looking forward to the day when I can leave Paris and never think of this house again."

A month passed and the house was still somber, cool with Séraphine's death, yet outside spring flooded Paris in a lagoon of blooming flowers. I still felt her presence, heard her voice call my name every time I passed through the foyer upon recognizing my footsteps from the boots she hated so much. I'd gone to plenty of funerals for people my family knew but none for someone I'd known as dearly as Séraphine, who'd talked to me like an old friend, offered me all her truths when she felt I needed them. Even though she'd likely distributed those same truths to a hundred girls who came before me, she let me believe I was as unique to her as she was to me.

Cato knew death. He understood it early in life from losing his mother, the bomb, and the threat of his illness. He took in Séraphine's death with solemnity, watching over me as I adjusted to her absence as though he knew, more than I did, that I'd have to learn this particular strength on my own for another day.

The loss of Séraphine bound the residents closer and we spent most days gathered together, conscious that our days as a group were coming to an end. I'd managed to convince my parents to let me stay an extra month into July, so I could witness the spectacle of the World Cup hosted by France. But just weeks later, we'd be locked out of the House of Stars. I'd no longer be able to speak to Maribel through the cottony wall that separated our bedrooms or fall asleep to the hum of Saira's TV overhead. There would be no more late-night bossa nova and cachaça-swigging fests in Tarentina's room and no more gossip sessions over breakfast in the dining salon, though the maids would be remaining in the house as employees of the new owners.

For the rest of the girls, there was the matter of making other arrangements, trying to piece together a future that would keep them from drifting apart. There was no apartment big enough to house more than a few girls. For some, letting go was easier. Saira announced that she'd move into her family's apartment on rue Royale; Stef wasn't allowed to visit her there but she said they'd figure something out. Dominique considered making a fresh start in London, and Maribel, who only had one year of school left until graduating, would room with a Mexican friend on rue Pergolèse while the others planned on taking an apartment together as close to our original address as possible.

Tarentina, however, toyed with the ideas of returning to Brazil though she had no family left, only a few childhood friends, or of finally letting herself be adopted by the Professor. She was end-lessly intrigued by the subject of my family, how my parents, two dispossessed children, had managed to create their own devoted clan, though she often teased that when I spoke of them, it sounded like I was speaking more of a cult than of a family.

She didn't know that, as a child, I'd often wondered what it would be like to be parentless like her. As a little girl, I'd been ter-rified of reliving my parents' painful past by becoming an orphan myself. Yet as I grew older, when passing a pair of panhandling New York runaways, or cast-off Bogotá street children selling gum at street corners, I'd indulged in a passing fantasy of being forsaken, wondering what it would be like not to be accountable to anyone else. I wasn't sure I would know what to do with that kind of freedom.

"I'll only tell you this once," Tarentina told me one May afternoon when I joined her for a cigarette on her terrace. "I really envy you. It must feel good to know you have a family waiting for you to come home. Sometimes I think the only person who will notice if I die is my accountant."

"I'll notice." I smiled.

"Will you?" She sounded less self-assured than I'd ever heard her.

"Of course. But you've got to promise not to disappear."

"You're the one who needs to make that promise."

I stared at the garden below us, the trees still decorated in candy-colored lanterns Saira had hung up for her design school's fashion show a few nights ago.

"If I had the money, I'd buy this place myself and keep it forever just the way it is now."

"Don't be stupid. I've been here five years and I do have the cash to buy it, but I wouldn't take this house if it were given to me. I'm afraid I'd end up like Séraphine, all alone in my bedroom with nothing but stories, guarding this house like it's a fucking fortress. You're free now. We all are."

"Do you think we'll all stay friends after we move out?" She knew better than I did how these things went.

"Some of us will keep in touch. Others will fade away. It's always like that."

"Really?"

"We'll see each other through weddings and children, I hope, and if there are divorces, we'll see each other through those, too. We don't need this house for that. Remember, they call this place the House of Stars, but *we* are the stars. Without us, it's just a house, and we'll go on being stars whether we live here or somewhere else."

* * *

If in Paris I was finding a slow peace, completing the last of my term paper orders for the girls ending their semesters, the windows of the house opening to the debut of summer, what I heard about my home in New Jersey was the opposite, imbued with creeping tension and anxiety because my little brother was declining, the positive effects of his latest treatment wearing off. He'd regressed to his occasional catatonic states, suicidal ideations, and refusal to speak to me when I called. My family hoped that my return would, at least temporarily, help to improve his condition.

I didn't want to burden Cato with these details, as if I could keep our own panorama pristine. But he heard my end of phone conversations with my parents and Santi, and even though we spoke in Spanish, he could see the trepidation on my face. As much as Tarentina proclaimed it, I was not free at all.

When we were kids, Santi and I used to say, even though we held dual citizenship, we were not American or Colombian. We were del Cielo, our own country. When we learned the pledge of allegiance in school, we made up our own pledge to our family. Ours was the only home I'd ever imagined knowing, and even now, I felt the pull on my heart.

Cato wanted me to stay.

One night in bed he'd said to me, "The way it happened between us, I don't think it could happen again with anybody else. Not like this. Do you?"

"No. Not like this."

He looked up at the ceiling and back at me on the pillow next to him.

"I don't want you to go."

"I don't want to go either."

I saw that he was beginning to depend on me in the way one depends on family, a love taking root beyond the early tumbles of new romance. I said, and believed, that I still had the choice and that I wanted to stay in France beyond my scheduled departure. For another year or two or forever. He believed me, too, even when my certainty slipped into negotiations: I could do both, return home for a while, then come back to France. I could live in both places. I could find a way to be everything to everybody.

Loic arrived at my door holding a small tissue-paper bundle like a pigeon in his hands.

"Gaspard and I have been going through our grandmother's things, you know, before the others start scavenging and leave us nothing to remember her by. We found this and thought you might want to have it."

He handed it to me and within its folds I saw Séraphine's silk kimono blouse with the dragon painted on the back.

I wore the blouse that night when Cato and I went for a walk to Île Saint-Louis, a bottle of wine in hand, settling onto the edge of quai Henri IV amid a crowd of lovers and friends. At nine in the evening the city was just beginning to darken, the Notre Dame lights radiating a golden sheen over the river. We found an abandoned padlock on an empty patch of concrete, probably fallen off one of the bicycles lining the quai. Cato decided to keep it. Later, when we started on our way home, we passed in front of the cathedral where painters and artists stood by easels offering cartoonish portraits to tourists. Cato asked one artist if he could paint our names on either side of the lock. The artist, who said she was an art student from Shanghai, used a tiny brush to print our names in yellow paint, and Cato held the lock by the tip of his fingers as it dried, and we crossed back onto the Left Bank, walking the long stretch from quai de la Tournelle to quai Voltaire, where Cato led me to the wall overlooking the water.

He held me, his face warm against mine.

"I want you to know that if you leave me you won't ever leave me."

"I'm not leaving you."

"But if you do go, it will be all right. We will both be all right."

He pulled apart from me and threw the painted lock with the most force I'd seen come out of those arms, so far across the water that it was impossible to know where it broke the surface.

He took my hand to his lips and kissed my palm.

"I think we should get married. Nobody would have to know. Just us."

"We already are married," I said, as if it were the most natural thing, and for that reason I knew it was true, in the only way that mattered.

16

Antoine de Manou's prior criticisms of the French national team became the mockery of every newspaper headline as the multiracial équipe Française ascended game by game through the World Cup to hero status. Romain's boss had a television installed over the bar at Far Niente, so we crowded around our favorite table along the wall to watch Brazil beat Scotland and committed to watch the rest of the tournament there together because there is a sporting tradition dictating that wherever you watch your favorite team play their first match is where you should watch all their games or you'll break the spell of luck.

The night that Les Bleus beat Croatia in the semifinal—a particularly humid one, with no air-conditioning in Far Niente, the doors and windows opened to let in the steamy street air—the restaurant crowd vibrated with jubilation, knowing it meant France would face Brazil, the defending champions, in the final. The Cup turns people into patriots, but as our teams, Colombia, the United States, Italy, and Morocco were knocked out in the early rounds, most of our allegiances shifted in support of our host nation, except for Tarentina, forever faithful to her Brazil.

Romain had the day off, but he still came back to the restaurant to watch the match with us. I sat between him and Cato, and when the match was over and we were on our feet, with victory chants and screams, he threw a bet on the table: If France won the Cup, he'd jump to his dream and book a flight straight to New York the next day.

We'd only come to the last pages of *Martin Eden* a few days before. I admired his tenacity—months of reciting each word slowly until there were no slips in his pronunciation and he glided through paragraphs and pages without needing to halt for my correction. He'd only stop himself when he became puzzled by a piece of the narrative, like how Martin could still love Ruth, even after she'd doubted him, questioning his poverty and dismissing his dreams of being a writer. He didn't understand how a man could love a woman who didn't believe in him.

"That's not love. Love is showing up every day, money or no money."

"She did love him." I found myself defending her. "But she had to make a choice. She trusted that her parents knew what was best for her."

"I'm repulsed by that type of woman. Mindless and spineless like a jellyfish."

"She thought *he* was the selfish one for being more devoted to his passion than he was to pleasing her and her family."

"She only wanted him back when he became a rich man. She was a coward. And so was he, for loving her for so long."

When he came to the end of the novel Romain lit us a pair of cigarettes relishing each word of the final page until there was nothing left to read. We were quiet, and when he was down to a nub of filter, Romain said, as if he'd given the matter serious thought,

"I can see why the guy killed himself rather than give her another chance. He was already dead. Me? I'd find another way to go on."

That night of the semifinal victory, everyone toasted Romain's vow to himself, and I wondered what it would take for me to wager my life on a match.

It was after midnight when Cato and I left the others in the street celebration that formed by the Odéon. Despite the noise of car horns and singing oscillating against the city walls, Cato and I walked home slowly, as if neither of us really wanted to arrive.

Les Bleus won the 1998 World Cup by three goals and the city didn't stop vibrating until after Bastille Day, one of the most climactic national celebrations in France's history; parades, crowds, and fireworks shows, a pedestrian ecstasy, marauding revelers flooding every inch of Les Champs-Élysées from La Défense to Place de la Concorde, down rue de Rivoli all the way to the Bastille, where the strong bodies climbed their way up the Colonne de Juillet, a blanket of pride covering the nation with its leaders proclaiming that this team of diverse faces represented the integrated dream of the future of France.

It would be a glorious, almost holy moment for the country. But by then, I would be gone.

17

Séraphine was right when she said good-byes don't serve anyone. We'd stayed up in Tarentina's room until near dawn, and when Cato and I returned to my room, the bed stripped of its sheets, I gathered the few things I had left to pack.

Cato helped the driver load my suitcases into his taxi, as I crept into each of the girls' rooms to hug them good-bye in their half sleep. I knew I'd see them all again.

I'd said good-bye to Loic early in the evening, thanking him for his kindness and for all he'd done to make me feel welcome in the house. I told him he was right, it was just as he'd promised, I'd been very happy there.

I stood alone in the foyer taking one long last look. I walked down the hall to Séraphine's room but found it had been locked and whispered good-bye through the door, hoping, wherever she was, she could hear me. I remembered when she used to say she'd outlived everyone she'd ever cared about, but it was no reason to feel sorry for her, because she'd loved so well in her life, passionément, à la folie, which is more than anyone should ever want from a life, and because, she told me, those you love deeply never disappear.

*   *   *

Through the help of one of Sharif's connections, Cato found what was likely the last available room in Paris in a quiet hotel in Montmartre, far from rue du Bac and all that was familiar to us. We wanted to spend our last day and night as tourists. We wanted to pretend we were a young couple coming to Paris for the first time, on our honeymoon, discovering the city through a small window with a view to a thousand chimneys, mansards, and alleyways. We fed bread crumbs to the pigeons on the small ledge of the balcony and soaked in the claw-foot tub.

I took Cato's water-shriveled hands in mine and showed them to him.

"This is how we'll look when we're old."

I didn't yet know, didn't yet understand, despite all the ways he tried to tell me, that he would never grow old the way I would. In that hotel room, we still played at a future together. He held me close, within his thighs, his arms tight around me as the bathwater turned cold, telling me that this winter he'd come visit me in the States. Or we could go somewhere else together. We could take a trip, to an island, to the other side of the world, to Leticia. He didn't care about the dangers to his lungs anymore. He was angry for the way he'd been raised to fear life and for accepting the limitations on his body. He didn't know how much life he had ahead of him but he wanted to run into it, fearless. He said he'd wasted too many years in that house by the sea. He didn't want to go back there now. Not without me.

I told him we'd do all the things he wanted to do.

We would go everywhere, together.

And I believed it.

I was still full of hope. I thought we had our whole lives ahead of us. I could do everything I needed to do and still find my way back to him.

I didn't yet know what was written for us.

The next morning at the Charles de Gaulle Airport I would run into Romain, who, as vowed, had booked a one-way ticket to New York and found an open seat on the flight after mine.

Within days of my return home, as long as it took to recover from the time difference and unpack my bags, I would be treated as if I'd never left. My family would stop asking to hear about my year abroad, and I would recalibrate, adjusting to the new anchor of home while remembering, only privately, my other homes: the little bedroom in the House of Stars and Cato's dark cavern in the house by the sea.

Instead of going back to school for diplomacy, I would become a teacher and build on my mother's volunteer efforts, the expansion of the philanthropic arm of Compa' Foods. I would look after my brother, see him through to his graduation and then college, help him find a new yet forever precarious stability in his routines.

I'd work hard. I'd believe I was content, productive. Useful. Fulfilled.

On most days I would feel I was doing all I'd been born to do. I would think of Cato often.

Those first years apart, we would write, call, and plan visits that would be postponed, rescheduled, and eventually canceled because some duty, some obligation on my part, would always interfere. I'd promise to go see him as soon as I could, as soon as my life allowed it, but my promises began to feel hollow, even to me.

Slowly, I would become more of a coward; gutless, pusillanimous like Romain's jellyfish, telling myself it was best to let the distance grow between us. It was the logical thing. I would tell my-self ours was a beautiful story but it must be over now. He couldn't possibly still love me. Not after all this time.

The years would unfold as Tarentina predicted. Some of the girls would hold on and some would let go. Five years after leaving, I would return to France for her wedding, and by then I would have convinced myself Cato had forgotten me and was living life contentedly with a woman better suited for him. I would eventually find a way to live mine with another man, an old college friend of my brother's, a political journalist with a pilot's license.

That night in the Montmartre hotel room I shared with Cato, I didn't yet know, or perhaps I did know, in some hidden part of my interior, that eleven years from now, in an apartment I shared with my new fiancé, I would receive a phone call that would ruin me for years.

I'd hear the voice of a woman asking me in French to hold the line for Monsieur Antoine de Manou. And then I would hear the voice of a very old man.

"Is that Leticia?"

"Yes, it is."

"Leticia, I am calling to inform you . . . of . . . of very unfor-tunate news."

I knew then. He didn't have to say more.

I felt my soul fall out of me.

"My son, Felix, has died. He was convalesced with a persistent bronchial pneumonia for several months. I am told by his doctors that he passed away in his sleep. The service will be this Friday for the family. In fact only Sharif and myself will be in attendance, with Mireille, who took care of him as a boy. With your permission

I will have my secretary arrange a plane ticket for you. I thought you should want to join us."

I was raw with shame for the ways I'd deserted him, and for the fraud of love I'd erected in his place.

To forgive myself, an impossibility.

There he lay before me once again, at the foot of the altar of La Madeleine, sleeping.

How arrogant and how naive to believe we'd had time when time is the one thing each of us has so little of.

That final night in Paris, he pressed his body far inside me, whispering into my ear, "I would give you everything if I had anything to give you."

"You already gave me everything. And you have all of me."

"Say you choose me."

"I choose you."

"And I choose you."

When we were through we studied each other's faces from across the pillow. I don't know if he'd felt the urgency as much as I did during those closing days in the pulsing pink summer of Paris, the compulsion to memorize it all then, as it would be a long time before I'd walk those streets again. I'd silently meditated on the finality of even the most insignificant things, like my last shower in the stark House of Stars bath, my last cigarette smoked on our terrace, the last time I dropped my laundry at the wash-and-fold across the way, and tried to ignore the heaving in my chest when Cato and I took our last trip to Blonville-sur-Mer, that last train back to Paris, and the final walk together over the smooth stone path of our bridge.

"You're beautiful," I said. "There is no one more beautiful than you."

He reached for my hand.

"You should have married me when I asked you to. We could have been married all this time. And you would leave me as my wife, and when you come back to me, I will still be your husband."

"I'll marry you now."

That night the Basilica of Sacré-Coeur was open and nearly empty except for a few prayerful people scattered in pews. It was ten o'clock at night, and I remember a short old man selling postcards and snow globes on the front steps warned us the church would be closing very soon.

We walked straight to the back of the church and found ourselves alone in the small chapel behind the altar. We said our vows. We said we chose each other. And we kissed with only statues as witnesses.

I left him the next morning lying in the mess of sheets, his skin pale against the white cotton. He watched me dress. A taxi waited on the street to take me to the airport, but I told him not to come along. I wanted to go alone. I wanted to remember him like this. His lips still fresh with me. With love in his eyes.

Acknowledgments

I am profoundly grateful to Ayesha Pande, Lauren Wein, Elisabeth Schmitz, Jessica Monahan, Deb Seager, and everyone at Grove for their kindness and very hard work. My thanks to all my family and the many dear friends, near and far, who've offered their continued support, especially the real girls of rue du Bac for whom this book was written with great affection as promised so long ago. My deepest gratitude and love goes to my brother, his family, and above all, to my parents.